DOTTED LINE

LOVE, CAMERA, ACTION #1

ELISE FABER

SNARKY BOOKS FOR SNARKY MINDS

DOTTED LINE
BY ELISE FABER

This is a work of fiction. Names, places, characters, and events are fictitious in
every regard. Any similarities to actual events and persons, living or dead, are
purely coincidental. Any trademarks, service marks, product names, or named
features are assumed to be the property of their respective owners, and are used
only for reference. There is no implied endorsement if any of these terms are
used. Except for review purposes, the reproduction of this book in whole or part,
electronically or mechanically, constitutes a copyright violation.

DOTTED LINE
Copyright © 2020 Elise Faber
Print ISBN-13: 978-1-63749-012-9
Ebook ISBN-13: 978-1-946140-53-1
Cover Art by Jena Brignola

LOVE, CAMERA, ACTION

Dotted Line

Action Shot

Close Up

End Scene

ONE

Olivia

"YOU CAN CHOOSE to prepare the files exactly as I've asked for them," I said, "*or* you can get the hell out of my office, get your shit off *my* desk, leave *my* building, and not come back."

My assistant, a burly six-foot-plus former athlete who'd decided to try his hand at managing instead of playing, glared at me. "I don't think your system—"

I sighed and tossed the file in the trash. "All due respect, Lane, it's not *your* job to think. *I'm* the VP because I know what I'm doing—"

"But—"

I stood, started to round my desk. "Moreover, this is the *third* time we've had this same conversation, and the previous two times I welcomed you to approach with changes you thought would benefit the company, but I also explained that I expected you to do so *after* you did things my way." I sighed. "You're fucking with my job. You're handcuffing me when we should be a team."

"You say team," he muttered. "But you don't let me have a voice."

"Did your coach let you have a voice when he was telling you to get on or off the ice?"

Lane's jaw worked. "He let us have input on plays."

"Yeah," I said. "And I'm still waiting to see writeups of those new, great ideas you have for plays here at Prestige."

He scowled. "I don't have time. The job is—"

"A lot." I crossed my arms, staring down at the peephole in my black pumps. "But also that's the job *you* signed up for."

I was unapologetically obsessed with my work, which meant I paid attention. It also meant I knew my assistant never got in before nine-thirty, never stayed past four, and always took at least an hour lunch break. Personally, I couldn't give two shits about his exact hours or how long it took him to eat his salad. All I cared about was the job.

Simple as that.

Do as I ask, and we didn't have problems.

Question, and while it *was* slightly annoying—I wasn't without ego. But I could put that ego aside and suck it up if it bettered the job.

Because I loved my job.

Repeat, I *loved* my fucking job.

And this lunatic had it in his head from day one that *he* knew better.

Look, I wasn't a total ass. I knew he *could* do some things better than me. Take a slapshot for one, skate around in that bulky hockey gear for another. I could finagle a puck near a goal without landing on my ass. But while he may know the sport of hockey, Lane didn't know the first thing about managing hockey *players*.

"The job is too much."

I sighed and glanced back up. "Lane, I've been patient here.

I know you aren't used to a nine-to-five, but I'm going to have to let you go if this persists. *This cannot happen again.* As it is, I'll be writing you up and speaking to Devon." I uncrossed my arms. "Now, please, get me the file the way I asked for it."

His shoulders were tense, his jaw like granite, but eventually Lane nodded and turned to leave, muttering something on the way out.

Since I wasn't stupid enough to think it was a positive comment on my abilities, I ignored it and turned back to my desk. Thanks to Lane's fuck-up, I was going to have to work late, which meant that I might as well get through some shit that was a lower priority.

The cold voice hit my spine before I made it to my chair.

"What did you say?"

Cole McTavish.

A tall hunk of a former hockey player, all muscled thighs and towering height, with a face that would have been classified as beautiful if not for the several-times-broken nose, the jagged scar along his jaw, and the small, smooth one bisecting his left eyebrow.

Further that, he was about as opposite from me as anyone I'd ever met.

Relaxed, always ready with an easy smile, Cole never raised his voice—at least *off* the ice. On it, he'd been a terror, a virtually unstoppable force who'd fought when needed and didn't back down from protecting a teammate.

I'd also been his agent while he was playing.

After he'd retired, I'd transitioned him over to Devon, who'd helped him refine his brand for post-playing opportunities. Now, he was the face for a few hockey companies and one well-known corporation that sold watches. Though, to my and the rest of the female populace's dismay, he'd turned down the swimwear ads.

I'd been with him in the locker room enough to know what was under those flannel shirts and jeans.

It was definitely billboard worthy.

Lane started to push by him, but Cole grabbed his shoulder and stepped into my office, forcing Lane back.

Devon Scott trailed them in, a stormy expression on his face.

I glanced at my boss and shook my head, silently telling him I'd already handled it, but Dev shook his head firmly back at me. Which was when I realized that what Lane had said must have been worse than I'd thought. Normally, Devon would never get involved in an argument between my employees and myself unless I asked him to.

Which I didn't.

Since I handled my own shit.

"Tell her what you said."

My gaze flashed to Cole and his darkened face. "It's—"

Emerald eyes locked onto mine, sparking fire. "Tell her," he said, and Lane must have realized exactly how deep of a pile of shit he'd dived into because when I broke Cole's stare to glance at my assistant, his face had gone pale.

I rested my hip against my desk. "I don't need to hear it. Lane, get the file."

Devon crossed his arms. "Tell her," he said. "If you're man enough to mutter it under your breath, you're man enough to say it aloud."

Lane shook off Cole and spun to face me. "Fine," he snapped. "I said that you're such a fucking bitch."

My lips curved and I huffed. "Okay, great, thanks. Now, back to work."

Lane's jaw fell open.

A curl of amusement crept onto Dev's face.

Cole appeared even more infuriated.

Lane somehow went paler. "Wh-what?"

"I've got a ton of work," I told him, "and you say bitch like it's a bad thing." I transferred my gaze to Cole and Dev. "*All* of you are acting like it's the worst insult in the world." I laughed. "Believe me, I've been called worse."

"It's unacceptable," Dev said, and I loved the guy for it.

But this was also the way of the world.

Most men despised strong women. We were told to smile or look happy or be fine with the scraps they tossed our way. If I'd had an issue with men calling me a bitch, I would have quit this male-dominated field ten years ago when I'd been a lowly assistant like Lane and my boss had been a lot worse than a bitch.

But I hadn't.

I'd put my head down, got my shit done.

And I'd learned to not give two craps when a man thought I was a bitch.

Because it had become my anthem.

When I negotiated my client to have equivalent perks in their contract, I was a bitch.

When I demanded a different client have access to the same off-season training as the rest of the team, I was a bitch.

When I secured a bonus that was similar to the rest of the big names on the roster, I was a bitch.

So, fine.

I was a bitch.

Great. Congrats. Moving on.

I turned my eyes back to Lane, who seemed to have shrunk two feet in the last thirty seconds. "I *am* a bitch," I said. "But I'm a bitch who gets her shit done. However, I'm *also* one who has no qualms about firing you, so it's time for you to get with the program or get the hell out." I lifted a brow. "You're replaceable, Lane. I want to make it so you're not, but you've got to work with me. If you don't . . ."

I purposely let the sentence trail for a few seconds then glanced at my watch.

"If you don't get me the Conner file by five, don't bother showing up tomorrow."

His eyes found mine again, and I honestly wasn't sure which way the tide would flow with that one. Ten-to-one he'd be gone in the morning.

Sighing, I gestured to the chairs in front of my desk as Lane left, thankfully cowed enough that he actually remembered to close the office door behind him. "I miss Becca," I told Dev.

Becca was his wife, who was currently on maternity leave. She'd become my assistant when she'd gotten together with Devon because HR rules applied even to executives.

"Not sure she'll come back," Dev told me. "She's really happy."

That didn't surprise me, nor did it disappoint, aside from the fact that Becca was one hell of a righthand woman. Motherhood fit for Becca. And while I wasn't the type of woman to stay home with kids and manage the day-to-day lives of a family, that also didn't mean I had any less respect for anyone who chose to do so. Hell, I had *more* respect for those making that choice in some ways because the job was hard, the hours never-ending, and I believed that women should have the option to do what made them happy.

Maybe that made me a bitch, too.

"Well, I'm not going to say that's *fine*," I grumbled. "But tell her she's still required to have lunch with me once or twice a month."

Dev's lips twitched, but he nodded. "You just want to see Jasper."

"The kid's growing like a weed," I said, not denying it.

Dev had been on paternity leave for the last six weeks but

had come into the office enough for me to appreciate all the cuteness of baby Jasper.

"Not surprising with a behemoth of a father like you."

"I'm proportional," Dev said, having heard that particular statement from me more than once, and settled into the chair. Cole followed suit, and I knew this meant the catching-up time had ended, and it was down to business. "Cole and I wanted to get your thoughts on a few opportunities, if you have time."

I smirked. "If I didn't have time, your butts wouldn't be in my chairs."

Cole chuckled and I watched as the fire left his expression.

Then couldn't decide if I were disappointed or relieved.

He crossed one leg over the other, jeans tightening over his thighs . . . no his *bulge*, they were tight over his bulge. *Act professional.* That's right, I needed to keep things professional, just like I had over the eight years he'd been my client. Cole was sexy, but he wasn't for me. He was good and kind and he lived on a ranch for half the year. I was barbed and closed off and wished Louboutin had a credit card.

Devon pulled out his cell, tapped the screen a few times, then began reading off terms of a contract for a car brand.

I glanced at Cole, eyes wide. "Holy shit, this is a big deal."

He shrugged, as was his way.

"Terms are shit," Dev said and kept reading, highlighting some truly shitty terms. "Cole doesn't really need the money, so it isn't like he's jumping to do these commercials," he said when he was done. "But this is a pretty big deal for a hockey player."

Dev was right. Especially in the States, these types of offers went to football or baseball players. Hockey just wasn't as popular. But understanding that it *was* growing and thus pulling in someone who had a face like Cole's along with a reputation for charity and hard work that made him known to people even outside of the industry, was a no brainer.

That they made the offer at all showed he had some power here.

Not a ton, but at least a smidge—and smidge specifically because I *only* used technical terms in my office. Ha.

"Do you want to do it?" I braced then allowed myself to look into Cole's eyes.

"For that amount of money?" He nodded at Dev's cell. "No. It's not enough to get me away from my horses." He sighed. "But I respect Dev's opinion—and yours, for that matter. If you guys think it's a good idea, I'll do it."

"Hmm."

I sat back and slipped off my fabulous red-soled shoes. Expensive or not, they weren't great for curling up in my fancy chair and pondering contract terms. Luckily, I was used to this being my best thinking position and so I wore wide-legged trousers that gave me maneuverability.

Didn't all women factor that into their clothing choices?

Pockets. Maneuverability. *Full-sized* pockets—worth mentioning separately because most of the time, the fucking pockets in women's clothing couldn't fit a penny, let alone a cell phone.

But I digressed.

Though my digressing in this case had the mutual benefit of sparking an idea.

"How about for charity?"

Dev had been in the middle of reading the terms for print and online ads but at my question, he stopped, a smile turning up the edges of his mouth. "Oh, that's good."

Cole glanced between the two of them. "What's good?"

"The money's shit, but we don't have a ton of negotiating power here because this isn't a normal offer for a hockey player, and even though the money isn't great, the exposure is enough they could find someone pretty easily." Dev pocketed his phone.

"But you don't really care about either money or exposure because you're fine with passing on the offer. The one thing you *do* care about, however, is the youth ranch, and if we bounce back saying the payment is going strictly to charity then we can bump up the payout, and they'll be more inclined to do so because they win two ways—it's a write off for taxes *and* they get to look like the good guys because they're partnering with a charity for underprivileged kids."

Cole froze, face blank, but I knew he was thinking, considering all the various ways this could play out. It was how he'd been on the ice, how he'd been with saving and investing and taking jobs during his playing career.

Then he spoke.

"How much do you think they'll donate?"

I named a figure.

He smiled.

And just like every other time he unleashed that fucking incredible flash of teeth and lips on me, I got wet.

TWO

Cole

"GREAT, I'll get those terms written up and sent over," Dev said and pushed to his feet.

I rose as well, shook his hand. "Gonna head back to the ranch. Call me if anything changes?"

"Yup." Dev nodded and Cole turned to thank Olivia, who was still curled up in her chair. I'd seen her in the same position many times over the years, always beautiful, always still as a statue. She wasn't a woman who wasted—time or movements or words. Though wasting money on those stupidly expensive shoes she wore was another thing altogether.

"Thanks, Viv," Dev called and left.

I turned back to the beautiful woman—inside and out despite the thorny, tough-as-nails exterior she liked to throw up between herself and the rest of the world. "I second my thanks, Olivia."

She threw me a businesslike, albeit distracted smile.

Already onto the next project, the next client then.

That stung a bit, just as it always had.

How was she able to make me feel like the only person in her life she gave a damn about, then it was done, and she was moving on to making her next client feel the same exact way?

Business. That was all it was.

Even if it felt like more.

"No problem," she said and picked up a file from her desk, eyes going to the papers inside. "Let me know if I can help further with it."

Dismissed.

Yeah, that was a familiar feeling.

"You ever feel like seeing the outside of this office," I said, heading for the door. "My barn door is always open."

"Cole?" She smiled over the papers. "That's never going to happen."

I raised a hand in farewell. "Never expected it to."

Her laughter trailed me out the door.

So fucking pretty and smart and kick ass . . . and not interested in me in the least. Stifling a sigh, I turned for the exit, thinking it was probably a good thing that her little piss-ant of an assistant wasn't at his desk.

Calling Olivia a bitch.

That had to be the most superficial description of the woman sitting in that office, and it showed that Lane had absolutely no clue how lucky he was to be working with Olivia Rogers.

Fucker probably also had no clue how lucky he was that Olivia hadn't fired his ass.

I reached the top of the stairs just as my phone buzzed. I pulled it out as I descended, which was probably why I missed the fact that Lane was coming up as I was going down. At least until he stopped in front of me and I nearly mowed him down. Even luckier for the bastard that I'd retained at least a few of my on-ice skills—mainly spatial awareness. Also lucky that my nose worked because the fucker smelled like he'd bathed in cigarette smoke.

"What's your problem, man?" he snapped.

Four steps from the bottom I sidestepped him and continued walking.

Yet another skill retained: ignoring little man-children who didn't know when to shut up and keep their heads down.

"You're a fucking snitch," he spat.

I kept moving.

"And she *is* a bitch."

I stopped.

"I don't care if she hears me say it."

Slowly, I turned. He'd had potential, I'd remembered that much. Good hands, good skater, lots of offensive capabilities. Not the best, but he'd been talented. A solid mid-roster guy, who should still be playing in the league. However, Lane's biggest obstacle to making it more than a few seasons in the NHL had been himself.

Bad attitude. Limited work effort.

He'd coasted along on his natural abilities until the pond had grown sufficiently large enough that the fish inside were bigger than him.

Then he'd floundered.

No pun intended.

"I don't care—"

I spun around, closing the distance between us in a heartbeat. Then I bent so my face was right in his. Not touching him, not putting my hands on him even, though I'd love nothing more than to pound Lane's face into a pulp. But I'd had a good agent and good opportunities because I didn't think with my dick. And I didn't need to prove mine was bigger than Lane's.

It was. That wasn't a question.

"You will not talk about her like that again," I growled.

He rolled his eyes and fuck, it was so hard not to grab him by the lapels of his cheap ass suit and shake some sense into him. Grinding my teeth at the same time as sucking in a breath, I tried to calm my voice.

"You're lucky to have a job here," I said. "Luckier still to have someone like Olivia teach you how to do it well—"

"I how—"

"You know jack shit," I spat. "And the sooner you figure that out, the better chance you'll have of keeping this job."

"I—"

Fuck this.

Without another word, I was gone.

Into the parking lot in an affluent part of the North Bay, my older model pickup truck looking very out of place when compared to the Lexus, BMWs, Mercedes, and the occasional Jaguar. Not like the rinks used to be when I was playing. Tricked out SUVs mixed with the odd Bentley and Maserati.

My truck had been nice then, with all the bells and whistles. The first new vehicle I'd ever bought myself. Also the last, because I just wasn't that into ruining a new one by driving it all over my ranch.

Gravel roads and fresh paint jobs didn't mix.

Neither did ding-free doors or unmarred undercarriages or—

I turned the key, thankful to stop my mental alliteration. The engine started with a roar—definitely *not* the purr of a sports car—and I backed out of the lot, turning in the direction of home.

Set more in wine country than ranch country, I still loved the fifty acres I owned in the heart of northern California. My house and horses were nestled amongst the beautiful rolling hills and oak trees, while the land I'd donated for the kids' ranch was filled with Redwoods and twisting creeks, with the sporadic glimpse of the Pacific Ocean and fog creeping in to keep the entire space cool.

I'd put an offer in on the land within ten minutes of first seeing the property, almost ten years ago. It had been everything I'd ever dreamed of, growing up as a poor kid in the big city.

Wide open space. Trees. Fresh air.

Yeah. Perfect.

It wasn't like I hated everything to do with cities or suburbia. I had a condo in San Francisco, enjoyed the restaurants, the way there always seemed to be something new to see or do.

But when I needed to escape—and that tended to be most of the time nowadays—I went to the ranch.

I rode my horses through the hills, sometimes camping out overnight and riding them all the way to the bluff on the edge of my property that overlooked the ocean. It was peaceful when I hadn't had a whole lot of peace in my life.

Still, I was starting to worry that I'd turned into a hermit.

Also, the reason I'd jumped into coming in person to the meeting with Devon rather than just Skyping in.

I'd been part of a team my whole life. It wasn't natural to be alone so much.

Lie.

Well, it was the truth, just not the *whole* truth. I was used to being on a team, sure. But I'd never been one of those guys who'd needed my teammates to function. I'd liked them, of course, but I'd treasured the opportunity for quiet time and space.

So, if I were going to be completely truthful, the reason I'd come to town was . . .

Olivia.

To see her because maybe she might—

Fuck. I'd been naïve in doing so, in thinking that maybe she might have finally realized I was a man she could see herself falling for or if not that then hoping the time I'd spent away from her had minimized my attraction. But instead I'd sat down in her office, in that chair on the opposite side of the desk, and I'd imagined knocking those files to the ground and fucking her on top of it.

Again.

Space hadn't done shit.

And she *still* wasn't interested.

I wasn't her client any longer, but she still looked at me with the detached professional interest she displayed with all of the players under her representation.

The heat, the need . . . it was all one-sided.

"Fuck," I muttered, taking the exit for the small highway that would twist and turn its way up to my ranch.

I needed to stop fantasizing about Olivia Rogers, needed to stop pretending that opposites attracted and that she was somehow holding on to a flame for me too. I had to realize that our lives were incompatible, and that even if she decided or, fuck, *gave in to* some secret urge hidden deep inside and figured out she was attracted to me after all, that she'd never be happy on the ranch.

And I couldn't be with a woman I couldn't share my whole life with.

I needed to get that through my thick skull and forget all about Olivia Rogers and her pretty smile, her gorgeous body, the lush lips always painted bright red, the black hair that hung silky and shiny down her back, the pale blue eyes that seemed to pierce right through me.

If only Olivia was a woman easily forgotten.

THREE

Olivia

THE FILE WAS on my desk at exactly five, and that meant my day ended on two disappointing notes.

First, I couldn't fire Lane.

Second, I was now working late.

Again.

Normally, I loved working late, being the last one in the building, everything quieting down so it was only me and the sound of my fingers on the keys of my computer.

But lately . . . I'd been unsettled.

Stupid. Or utter hogwash, as my granny used to say.

That, at least, made me smile. She was part of the reason I was a ballbuster, my granny. She'd been a real-life Rosie the Riveter during World War II, helping to build some of the huge ships in the Kaiser shipyards off Alameda. No fear about stepping into a "man's" job, or at least if she'd had fear, she'd never let it slow her down. And she'd continued living without fear. She became the breadwinner for the family after my grandfather had suffered a devastating heart attack at a young age, beat

Stage Four colon cancer, and lived a full life after all that and the premature death of her husband.

A full life filled with trials and obstacles.

So, I'd had no choice but to overcome mine.

And also to become extremely competitive at board games because my granny didn't like to lose. At anything.

Funny.

Wonder where I got that particular attribute?

Smirking, I picked up the file, kicked my shoes off, and curled into my chair. The folder in question contained all things Billy Thomas, potential new client, rising up-and-comer in the NHL, and what appeared to be an amazing personality both on and off the ice.

Humble. Confident with the occasional quotable sound bite. Good-looking.

The perfect client.

But I hadn't gotten as far as I had by allowing myself to be taken in by a pretty face and good sound bite.

I researched. I vetted. And I researched some more.

Not to say I didn't miss something, but that research paired with my instincts—I *never* ignored my instincts—meant that I was very choosy about the clients I was bringing into Prestige Media Group.

One might reasonably ask why then I chose Lane to be my assistant.

Well, even though I'd been asking the very same question myself earlier that day, I also knew the kid had potential. I'd known about the chip on his shoulder when I'd hired him, knew that he tended to get in his own way more often than not. I just assumed . . .

Here was *my* ego talking.

Because I assumed that *I* could be the one to get that plank of wood off his shoulders.

Now he was on chance three.

And I didn't give more than three chances.

Sighing, I focused on the papers in front of me and started reading. Usually, the first read-through was superficial on my part, skimming and storing the useful bits of information, filtering out the others, relying on my instincts to see if something did stand out to me. It was engrossing.

Also, probably why I didn't hear Dev until he was on the other side of my desk.

"Hey," he said, and I jumped, almost toppling out of my chair.

Which made him laugh, the ass.

"Hilarious," I muttered, stretching my neck so I could see the clock on my computer screen. I'd been engrossed in all things Billy Thomas for the last two hours.

"From my vantage point, it was," he said and plunked himself down into my chair. "Why are you still here, Viv?"

"Lane."

He lifted a brow.

"What?" I asked.

"Why are you here?"

I rolled my eyes. "In an existential crisis sense or why am I still in the office? If it's the first, then it's because we've evolved from apes to take over and ruin the Earth and my ancestors decided to contribute to the overpopulation problem. If it's the second, then it's because Lane got me the file at the end of the day, and I needed to stay late to go over it."

"Dark," he said and crossed one leg over the other. "I'm sure it did something to *his* bulge, but my eyes weren't drawn there in the least.

Le sigh.

Even when he wasn't there, Cole still colored my thoughts.

"When's the meeting with Thomas?" Dev asked.

I hesitated. "End of the week."

"So, it's Monday. Why are you staying late today?"

"If I don't get this done today," I said. "I'll get behind."

"Will you really?"

I sighed. No. I probably wouldn't. Friday afternoon was a long way from Monday. But—

"Why are *you* still here?" I asked.

"*I'm* leaving," he said.

"And yet, still here, pestering me in my office."

He sighed and pushed to his feet. "I'm going. But Viv, I see you. Not sure why you're hiding from life by working all the time—"

"I—"

"Not judging," he said, lifting his palms. "But as a person who spent many years in the exact same state, I'll just say that I'd love for you to find your own bit of happy."

"I *am* happy."

"Noted." He waved, headed for the door.

"They counter yet?" I asked.

"Yup."

I waited for him to tell me about the offer for Cole. When I realized he wasn't going to, I asked archly, "And?"

He paused. "They'll play ball," he said and flashed me a smirk. "I'll tell you about it at a reasonable hour." A beat. "Tomorrow."

"Hilarious," I called, watching his retreating back, knowing he was looking forward to seeing Jasper and Becca. He deserved that, deserved a happy ending, and so did Becca.

They both deserved a lifetime of contentment.

They were worthy of finding that fictional happily ever after in real life.

I wasn't cold-hearted. I wouldn't pass up a happy ending.

The difference was that I knew one wouldn't find me.

Sighing, I curled back up in my chair and flipped to the next page.

I'D LEARNED that men aren't the only ones who resent strong women right around the same time I learned that I was bossy and too abrupt and far too outspoken for my place in the world.

I learned this over time and throughout my interactions in school, but I had the last driven into me by a particularly nasty female teacher in elementary school.

Questions weren't allowed.

And I raised my hand far too often to be allowed to answer hers.

I should let others have a turn.

Also, a boy was never going to be interested in me if I kept taking all of the attention. I should step back and let them have their fair share of it.

Of course, that fair share was *most* of it.

Attention hadn't been something I was after at the time. Or not in the way that the teacher had thought. I'd been proud to know the answer, happy that I was smart. Brains had been celebrated by my granny, by my father, and as much as I'd never wanted to be like my mother, I had definitely wanted to be smart and tough like my grandma. My granny never let being a woman stop her from doing anything, I remembered that fiercely, even though she passed just a few months after my father.

I'd lived in this blissful existence until they were gone thinking that I could be anything I wanted to be, if only I worked hard enough, that the outside world had little bearing on my trajectory if I *just kept pushing*.

Oh sure, I'd been called bossy or a know-it-all, but those weren't bad words to me.

I was independent. Strong. Like my grandma. And those were *great* things.

But with one interaction, *one* time being kept after class to give me some "advice," that teacher had broken something inside me.

And my mother had stomped on those pieces by pulling me out of school. I was too loud, too disruptive to be in a classroom, and so for the sake of the teacher and the other students, I couldn't be *allowed* to go back.

But in reality, it was a punishment, moving away from everything I knew, being isolated, hearing the litany of negative things about me day in and day out. I'd competed with my father's attention, taken something from *her*, and so once he was gone, I'd needed to be taught a lesson.

I'd once been all of these great things my grandma and father respected . . . and yet it didn't matter to my mother. I was a failure.

I could be independent and strong and smart, *or* I could be worthy of those around me. I could be tough and brilliant, *or* I could be a pathetic, spiteful, lonely individual whom no one saw any value in.

Looking back, I couldn't be ashamed for having retreated, for getting small and quiet while those words had cut at my soul.

I regretted it to this day, however.

I'd let them change me, solely because they'd sized me up and thought I was unworthy.

Not any longer.

Eventually I'd found my way back to strong.

"Great," I muttered, standing up from my chair and stretching out my aching back. The file Lane had pulled together was just as I'd requested. Finally. And my initial read-through had only thrown up a couple of items I thought warranted a deeper look. Which meant that I was done for the night.

My heels went back on, along with my coat. My laptop went into my bag because it was my life and I never went anywhere without it. Then I turned out the lights before heading for the stairs.

Steph was coming up, a vacuum in one hand, headphones around her neck. "You're out early," she said, smiling at me.

It was our routine, no matter how late I came across her. Sometimes I missed her altogether because she didn't vacuum this floor if I was holed up in my office, just kept to the ground level and hit the offices the next night.

I grinned. "Want me to go back and work some more?"

She rolled her eyes. "Don't think that's possible, coming from you, Viv."

"Meh," I teased. "I'm sure I can find something to keep me busy."

"Shoo," Steph said, indicating the front doors with the vacuum. "Find *someone* to keep you busy. *I've* got work to do."

And considering she *did* have work, I nodded and kept walking. "Tell Sam I said hi."

"Will do," she said, already at the top of the stairs and unwinding the cord.

Sam was her son, a precocious six-year-old with adorable blond curls. He was also the reason she worked so hard. A single mom who took care of her mother and son by owning a cleaning business for residential clients during the day and businesses at night.

"Oh!" I called, "There's an envelope for him on my desk. Says Sam on it."

"*Olivia.*"

Shit.

I stopped and glanced back at the woman who was very close to my age but always managed to pin me in place with a stern tone and a stony look. "Only thing on there," I told her. "You can't miss it."

A beat then, "*Viv.*"

And they said *I* was the bitch.

But that thought made my lips twitch. "I got some tickets to some videogame YouTuber thing. They were free," I added, even though they weren't. "I'm certainly not going to use them. You guys might as well go and enjoy yourselves."

"Maybe if it wasn't something to do with gaming or YouTube, I could."

"You're welcome," I teased, then sent her a salute and continued my trek to the front doors.

"Viv."

"Yeah?" I asked, fingers on the handle.

"You don't need to look after us," she said. "But thanks for doing it anyway."

There were a dozen things I could say to that, but they all sounded cheesy or inauthentic in my head, so instead I settled on, "You're welcome."

Short. Sweet. Punchy.

Exactly how I liked my alcohol.

Speaking of which, it was time to get a move on. I had a pair of shoes to take off, pajamas to slip into, and a cocktail to mix up.

Then I was going to turn on *Netflix* and veg.

By myself.

Exactly how I liked it.

Even if by myself was just the teeniest bit lonely.

FOUR

Cole

THERE WAS nothing better than the breeze on your face.

I'd felt that way from the time I was a little kid. Cool air coming off Puget Sound in Seattle. The frosty chill when stepping out on the ice. The wind tugging at my hair as I stopped on the bluff overlooking the ocean.

I slid from the saddle and ground-tied Bucky, letting him have his head so he could graze while I sank down and settled in to watch the sunset. I'd camp there that night, letting the crashing of the waves settle over me. Buck liked it too, getting out of the ranch, being able to stretch his legs through the long, winding paths.

Fine.

Truth was, *I* liked it.

I liked the freedom and the ocean, the tang of salt in the damp air.

I'd just been too busy to enjoy it for the last month.

The car company had come back with an offer, doubling their money and committing to make a permanent yearly donation to the youth ranch. It was generous, too good to pass up, and so I signed on the dotted line.

Then I had spent the last thirty days either meeting with wardrobe people or memorizing lines or getting my hair styled— fucking ridiculous, the lot of it—or I'd been at the ranch, supervising construction and hiring staff and working with members of the board I'd brought in because they knew how to run a charity, and I wanted my job to be less day-to-day and more in name.

I also wanted to make sure it would last, and it could be run without me.

Because one day, it *would* be.

Morbid? Maybe. But I wasn't immortal, and I knew well enough that bad stuff could happen without warning.

The end effect was that after a month of work, everything was more manageable, money was secured in a trust for the ranch, and we had a good, background-checked staff in place.

"So, now what?" I muttered, leaning back against a rock.

Another goal met, another life's dream under way.

And. Now. What?

I stared at the waves, their frothy tops flipping over, coating the navy in white foam. They pounded against the beach that was more rocks than sand below. I watched them roll in, covering the rocks, turning them almost black in the waning light. Less than thirty minutes before sunset, night was tucking in around me.

Perfect.

Isolated.

Lonely.

Shoving the thought away, I'd turned to grab my tent from Bucky's back when I saw it.

A shadowy creature floating across the sliver of sand.

She walked gracefully, and my breath caught as the breeze

pulled at her clothes, tugging them against her body in such a way that I knew it was a her. Dark hair whipped around her face, and I watched her struggle with it for a second before bending to set a pair of shoes on the sand. Then she did that intrinsically female thing—looking out at the distance while instinctively pulling back and securing her hair. I'd always thought the action was sexy, a little peek into a woman's life when she didn't think people were watching. It also didn't hurt that the action was unintentionally sensuous, thrusting out her breasts, arching her spine—

So, I was occasionally a pig.

But it was actually a good thing I was watching so closely.

Because otherwise, I would have missed her falling.

It happened between one split second and the next. She was balancing on one foot, preparing to stretch the other for a rock when the wave hit.

With a shriek, she lost her balance and went seesawing through the air, legs up, arms scrabbling, and water washing over her. I stiffened, waiting for her to get up, seeing her struggle, but then another wave came crashing in.

That's when I moved.

I bolted for the winding path that led down to the beach, rushing over the steps intermixed with cliffside, plants, and sand, all while knowing I was less than thirty feet above her, but also that the distance between us seemed interminable now that I was hurrying to cross it.

Finally, my boots hit the sand, and I ran across the surface.

My hands grabbed one arm, the other flailing for a moment before I wrapped my fingers around a slender wrist.

And then I pulled, yanking her up and out of the swirling wash of water, thinking it was lucky she'd landed the way she had, otherwise I'd be cleaning up blood. As it was, the current was strong, she was soaked, her clothes weighing her down, and it took every bit of my strength to wrestle her up and away from the incessant waves without ending up in the little crater myself.

"Hang on," I told her, stepping carefully through the rocks to a safer stretch of the beach.

"My—" She coughed. "Wait." Another cough. "My shoes."

Brows drawing together, I glanced at the pair of heels abandoned in the sand, their red soles evident even from a distance. My eyes flew to the bundle of woman in my arms.

Black hair.

Lush body I'd been attempting to ignore.

Red, *red* lips.

"Olivia?" I nearly dropped her where we stood.

Her eyes widened, showing off those gorgeous blue irises. "Cole?"

"What are you—?"

A huge wave crashed into the rocks behind us, loud enough that we both jumped, and I was reminded of the fact that we were on a narrow stretch of beach in the middle of nowhere with the tide coming in.

"Hang on," I said, plunking her down on the sand while I retrieved the shoes she was obsessed with. A moment later I was back, tucking them into her shivering lap before I lifted her in my arms again.

She made a noise of protest, starting to stiffen.

"Shush," I said sharply, surprising myself with my tone. I was never sharp, but she was shivering and wet, night was falling, and we were on what was turning out to be a dangerous outcrop of beach.

I must have surprised Olivia, too, because she didn't protest further—or shockingly, argue with me. Instead, she clutched her shoes with shaking fingers and let me carry her back up to where I'd left Bucky and my supplies.

Thankfully, Bucky was a well-trained horse and hadn't wandered off.

I set Olivia on a rock then grabbed my pack, pulling out a large towel to wrap around her. "Your car here?"

There was a parking lot about a half-mile down the road.

"Yeah," she said. "Not at the lot though. At the barn."

I frowned. "The yellow one or the old one?"

"If the old one is the pile of logs somewhat resembling a barn, then that one."

"That's over a mile back."

She shuddered. "I know. Engine died."

"Fuck," I muttered. "You hit your head?"

"No."

"Anything injured?"

"N-no," she said through chattering teeth. "J-just cold."

That was lucky, at least. I never brought my cell on rides like this. Stupid now that I thought about it. This *was* California, but there were still venomous snakes and mountain lions. Not to mention it was getting dark and it would be pretty convenient to be able to call down to the ranch for someone to pick us up.

I grabbed the pack on Buck's other side and started pulling out my tent.

"It's going to be pitch black here in a few minutes," I said. "I need to get this set up.

"A-and st-start a-a f-fire?"

I shook my head. "That I can't do. Burn ban," I added when she glanced up at me in confusion. "But I can get you some dry clothes and a place to stay for tonight."

"St-stay?" she asked.

Ignoring the question because I didn't have time for an argument, I began pulling out clothes. Sweats, boxers, socks, a fresh shirt, a heavy flannel, a sweatshirt. I might have played hockey and been used to sweating in the cold, but it was a completely different feeling sleeping next to the Pacific out here. The cool temperatures had a way of permeating multiple layers.

So, I came prepared.

"Strip," I told her.

"What?" she exclaimed. No chattering this time, but her skin had taken on a bluish tinge I didn't like.

"I won't look. Promise," I said. "The only thing those wet clothes will get you is hypothermia." Then I set the dry clothes in front of her and returned to the pile that was the tent and started to put the poles together.

I expected an argument, but I'd meant what I'd told Lane before.

Olivia was smart and tough *and* logical.

If presented with something she didn't agree with but it made logical sense, she would consider it fully then implement as necessary. In this case, it *was* necessary she change clothes because freezing her ass off on a cliff overlooking the ocean wasn't an efficient use of that gorgeous brain of hers.

I heard the plunk of something sodden hit the rock then several others, but I kept working on the tent, sliding the poles through the channels while simultaneously trying to ignore the fact that Olivia Rogers was probably naked behind me at that very moment, and I was thinking of poles and channels.

"Do you have your phone?" she asked. "Mine died a watery death courtesy of the waves."

I finished with the poles then began on the stakes. "No," I admitted. "I don't bring one when I go riding."

Silence.

I turned, brow raised, never knowing her to pass up an opportunity to give me shit when I was doing something stupid.

"What?" she asked, popping her head through the sweatshirt like a whack-a-mole.

"Nothing."

"I'm not going to say it's stupid," she said, "because you already know it's stupid not to have a cell in case you break your dumb neck on that horse of yours." A sigh. "I'm also not going to say it's stupid for me to be climbing over rocks in bare feet and work slacks after leaving my car on the side of the road to wander through a countryside that I'm unfamiliar with."

Well, put it that way.

I smirked.

"Shut up," she snapped, picking up her clothes and laying them on the rock to dry out. I tried and failed to ignore the fact that the red lace matched her lipstick.

Pervert.

Maybe.

But damn was Olivia sexy.

"You warm enough now?" I asked, reaching for the sleeping bag and pad I had on Bucky's back. She nodded as I spread them out in the tent then went out to take care of Buck, spreading some hay on the ground before filling a bucket at the freshwater stream between the trees.

Once that was done, I returned to see her sitting on a rock, staring out at the horizon.

"Why were you out here anyway?" I asked, reaching into my pack and pulling out a couple of protein bars and peanut butter sandwiches. I didn't exactly live it up with gourmet meals while out here, but at least I had some food to offer her.

"You mean, why am I out in nature when I obviously repel it?"

I grinned. "Or piss it off?" I teased, remembering how the almost angry waves had taken her down.

"I refuse to anthropomorphize nature." She said, lifting her chin.

"This is from the woman I once saw give a lizard a top hat?"

"It was a toad." She tore off the wrapper of a bar and took a bite. "The alliteration makes it funnier," she said, after chewing and swallowing. "But the toad was your teammate's pet, so it wasn't really nature."

I raised a brow, lips twitching. "Does a toad not come from nature?"

"Technically, I believe it came from a pet store," she said. I snorted. She laughed then bumped my shoulder. "Thanks for the assist. I was really scared there for a second."

I was tempted to dismiss her words with an "It was nothing," or a "No problem," but I knew her, knew she was being sincere, so I just went with a simple, "You're welcome," and watched her blue eyes warm from the inside out. "Should we circle back to my previous question? Are you going to tell me why you were out in the middle of nowhere, stumbling around in your Louboutins?"

"I resent that statement," she said, starting in on the peanut butter sandwich. "I do *not* stumble on my Louboutins. I saunter."

"Noted."

Because she did saunter.

And it was a damned fine sight to see. That was for sure.

"So, why were you sauntering?"

Blue eyes met his, a touch of heat in their center. "I was looking for you."

My heart skipped a beat, a slow grin curved my lips, my cock twitched.

Fucking *finally*.

FIVE

Olivia

FOR A SECOND, I swore I saw heat in Cole's eyes, but then I kept talking and realized that I must have been mistaken.

No heat was there.

Not for a city girl who wore heels to a dude ranch.

Fine. Not a dude ranch. A *youth* ranch.

"Jasper is sick, so Devon asked if I could call you about some other opportunities."

His blond brows drew down. "Is Jasper okay?"

I nodded. "Just a cold, but he's little and Dev is a first-time dad." I shrugged, remembering the worried look in my friend's eyes and how even though I'd ordered him to go home and be with Becca and Jas, that he hadn't fought me very hard.

He had a life, and his job hadn't gotten in the way of him living it.

Maybe that was why I'd come up here.

I'd called Cole's phone, and instead of leaving it until he called me back—like I would have done *any* other time in the past that I'd reached out to him with career opportunities—I'd left the office early and driven up here.

Early for me, of course.

Since I hadn't actually headed out until close to seven, but that had been a good thing, traffic-wise. I'd cruised—mostly—up the highways, had been enjoying the way the scenery seemed to stretch out in front of me for miles and miles. Funny, that. I'd never imagined I would have missed wide, open stretches of land, not after having grown up in the middle of nowhere.

I liked my easy access to mani-pedis. Loved Amazon Prime delivery and DoorDash and Instacart. I liked nice clothes, heels, makeup.

And yet . . . I stifled an internal sigh.

I kind of liked this, too.

"Must be terrifying."

For a second, I thought he meant me nearly dying in the ocean, the rush of water slamming over me, pinning me down to the sand. My pulse picked up at the memory, and I knew I'd never hear the crash of the waves in the same way. That beauty would always be tempered by deadly force.

But I was fine.

Safe.

Felt a bit like I'd been pulled backward through a hedge, but I was . . . fine.

Just like always.

I blinked away the waves, the fear, shoved them both deep, *deep* down, and turned to Cole. "W-what must be terrifying?"

He froze, studied me for a long moment. "You really okay?"

Yeah. So not going there. "Fine," I said brightly.

More freezing. More of his eyes studying mine before he sighed, as though deciding he wasn't going to battle me to dig the thought out of my mind.

Probably because he knew by now that was impossible. I

was a stubborn bitch and no amount of pushing, cajoling, or pressuring would do anything aside from getting me to dig my heels.

"Suddenly becoming wholly responsible for the well-being of another person," he said instead of trying to get me to talk.

My lips twitched. "Especially one who can't even hold his head up."

"That, too."

We sat for a few minutes in companionable silence, during which I wrapped my head around the fact that I was in the middle of nowhere, it was nearly dark, and the only reasonable accommodation around was a tent.

And one sleeping bag.

I'd noted that, too, right around the time I'd downed the protein bar, not having realized how hungry I'd been and how grateful I was that Cole had shared. But I had a predicament.

Cole was my predicament.

"Why didn't you just call?"

See? *That* was why Cole was a quandary, a mental and physical quagmire. I was attracted to him, and not just his body. His brain was sexy, too, as was his ability to see through the bullshit I was painting.

Jasper was sick, of course. I wouldn't lie about that.

But I'd been hoping to avoid the actual reason for my little jaunt up into the rolling hills. Frankly, I wasn't ready to admit it to myself yet, preferring to pretend it was work that brought me up, and not suddenly that I'd had the urge to jump in my car and scratch an itch that was all things Cole.

My obsession.

I'd just gotten so damned good at pretending it didn't exist that I'd forgotten how strong it was.

I never acted on my attraction to Cole, of course. He was a client.

And I was . . . me.

When the yearning got bad, I carved myself a slice of time with him, whether it was a two-minute phone call or a visit after practice when he'd still been playing. After he retired and I'd passed him off to Dev, it had gotten easier.

Who said that cold turkey wasn't an effective way to beat an addiction?

Morons, clearly.

Since I was there in that moment. Ha.

It was just . . . this date.

This anniversary. My father had died more than two decades ago and—

The pain, it never fully went away—

"You okay?" he asked, hand resting lightly on my forearm.

I pulled away. No touching. No handshakes or hugs. I couldn't. Not with Cole. I still felt his arms around me from earlier, and having him touch me gently as well was just too . . . I sighed internally . . . *too much*. Still, I forced a smile to take a sting out of my action.

"I had business up here, actually," I lied, turning my eyes toward the ocean, even though I could now barely make out the white tips of the waves.

He studied my profile for a long moment, long enough for me to think that he was going to buy that fib. But then he proved why I liked him so much when he said, "Lie."

"What?"

He shoved to his feet and touched a finger to my soaked clothes. "Those aren't going to dry overnight," he muttered before glancing down at me. "I know when you're lying, Olivia. You do this thing with your mouth."

I immediately relaxed my lips. "I don't know what you're talking about."

He sighed. "Is there a problem with the commercials?" A

beat. "With the donation? Did you come up to break it to me gently?"

I jumped to my feet and winced, the movement reminding me I'd been assaulted by a wave earlier. Cole reached out as though he were going to steady me then stopped, probably based on the way I'd acted a few minutes before.

God, he was such a good guy.

And that wasn't me.

I wasn't good.

Still, I moved a little closer, wanting him to see my face, to see I wasn't lying. "No," I said. "This isn't about the commercials or the donation. They're both good. This is truly about a few offers that Dev has for you because the ads are going well, and other companies are interested. They're smaller offers, but worth listening to." I shivered when a breeze picked up, shoving my hands into the pocket of the sweatshirt. "But the real reason he wanted me to make contact, and to do it soon, was because the Gold would like to bring you in as a guest commentator for a few games this season, and if you do decide you want to go for that, a decision has to be made by Monday."

Silence, then, "Because the season's starting soon."

I nodded.

"I don't have much interest in commentating. Would they be willing to discuss different positions?"

"What did you have in mind?"

"Player development?" he asked. "Something with their youth programs?" A shrug. "I like helping out kids who don't have a lot of opportunities."

Because he'd once been a kid who hadn't had many opportunities.

And with a little support, he'd gotten *here*.

"Those positions don't pay a lot," I felt obliged to point out, shifting from foot to foot.

He bent and adjusted one of the stakes on the tent. "So, you came out here to talk about my salary?"

Shit.

"Well, like I said, I was in the area."

He straightened, voice dropping. "And like *I* said, *that's* a lie."

"Look, asshole," I snapped. "You don't know what's going on in my mind, okay? Nor do you have any bearing on where I go or when I do it. If I felt like taking a jaunt up to Tahoe to get a cone of ice cream, I could. If I want to buy another overpriced pair of heels just because I like the color, I—"

"I like your heels."

I froze. His voice was soft, but almost predatory, raising goose bumps on my arms and leaving me struggling to find the rest of my rant.

My eyes locked with his.

This time there was no missing the heat in their depths.

I shivered again.

"You're cold," he said, switching topics so abruptly that I scrambled to keep up. "You should go in the tent. Zip up. I'll sleep out here tonight."

It took me a moment to process his words, but then my brain started working again. Finally. Cole was turning me into a pathetic, unthinking lump. "You can't sleep outside!" I tugged the hood of the sweatshirt up and crossed my arms. "It's already freezing out here."

My eyes had adjusted enough to the waning light that I saw his eyes spark with irritation. Or maybe it was irritation mixed with heat?

Either way, I wasn't going to back down.

He was the client, and his comfort was paramount.

"I'll sleep out here."

He huffed and crossed his own arms. "Olivia. Get in the tent."

"Yeah, no, Cole. Not happening."

A glare that should have skinned me down to my bones. "Look, *I'm* not the one who's shivering with about ten layers on. Nor am I the one who got dunked in the ocean."

"Your clothes got wet, too," I snapped.

He held his hands out. "And yet, no shivering."

"God, you're annoying."

A snort. "Right back at you."

"I—" That damned cold breeze came up again, whipping around my wet hair and making my teeth start chattering.

"Olivia."

"I'm not going in the t-tent," I said and stamped my foot.

Yes. Stamped it.

Then immediately winced because the ground was hard and cold and, of course, I'd managed to stomp my sole down on a rock.

"Why are you so stubborn?"

"It's in my fucking DNA."

And it was. Right in there with holding a grudge and never admitting I was wrong. My mother had taught me many things.

Before disowning me, but that wasn't really the point in this moment.

Cole was close enough for me to see the lines forming between his eyebrows. "Stubborn," he said. "And beautiful. So fucking beautiful it makes my heart skip a beat anytime I'm within thirty feet of you."

His voice hadn't changed, and so it took me a few seconds to process the words he'd spoken.

"Wh-what?"

He took a step closer. My breath caught.

"I've always thought you were the most gorgeous woman I'd ever seen."

"I—"

Another step closer. I could smell him now, spicy, and male, and intoxicating.

"And smart. So fucking smart that I sometimes feel like an idiot around you."

That made me frown.

"Cole—" I began, but he cut me off by saying, "Brilliant. Fucking hilarious. Tough as hell."

Words stoppered up in my throat.

I didn't know what to say to that.

I liked Cole, had been lusting after him for ages, but he'd never given me any indication that he'd done more than tolerate me. I'd always assumed I was a necessary evil in his life, someone to steer his career when he was more interested in playing and doing his charity work.

Shaking my head, I slid a step back. "It's the ocean air," I said.

He took a step forward. "Nope."

"Hero complex then."

"Not that either."

My eyes cut to the side, saw the tent, knew it was my only escape. "I've changed my mind," I said. "I'll take the tent."

His chest brushed mine, head lowering until I felt his next words against my lips.

Too bad they sliced right through me.

"Running, Vivie?" he asked, lids half-mast, eyes hot, lips so close.

What I wouldn't have given for him to kiss me.

But he'd called me *Vivie*.

And nothing could have reminded me so effectively of our differences. Every single one of them. A man who was interested in helping others more than himself, who rescued people without hesitation, who offered dry clothes and tents, who saw a woman who might be pretty on the outside but . . . wasn't good on the inside.

Vivie, I heard my mother's voice as clearly as though it were spoken directly in my ear. *Why were you born so bad?*

I reared back, eyes stinging, but I couldn't let him see.

Couldn't let *anyone* see a softness, a weakness to exploit.

I had to be surrounded by steel and spikes and barbed wire.

"Olivia?" He caught my arm when I spun away.

My reaction was instinct, and I would be horrified for it later. But it also was more proof of the bad, of the unkind, of me being rotten to my core.

I spun back to face Cole, my arm coming up, and—

Smack.

My palm collided with his cheek.

His expression darkened. His hand released me.

I ran for the tent, zipped myself in, and threw myself down onto the sleeping bag, knowing with a surety down into my bones that I'd just ruined one of the few good things I had in my life.

I should have never come here.

SIX

Cole

I STARED at the silent tent, my cheek stinging, for a long time.

What the fuck had just happened?

No, seriously.

What *the fuck* had just happened?

Sighing, I went over to check on Bucky, making sure he was tied off, so he wouldn't wander off into the woods, then took an inventory of my packs. A pillow I hadn't had a chance to put in the tent, an extra blanket, my jacket, a few hand warmers.

It was going to be a cold-ass night.

But it wasn't the cold air that was filling my insides with frost. It was the look on Olivia's face when I'd called her Vivie.

Devastation.

Absolute, soul-crushing devastation.

What the hell was that?

Dev called her Viv with regular frequency, so did most of her other clients. The only reason I hadn't was because I'd worried if I'd broken the barrier—first name to nickname—that I'd forget she was supposed to be my agent.

And not my woman.

I'd needed that mental distance

She wasn't interested in me that way—or so I'd thought. Now, I wondered if I'd been missing something critical for all these years.

Dumbass, of course you've been missing something critical.

Why did my mental critic always sound like Olivia?

Probably because I hadn't been able to get her off my mind for the last eight years.

Sighing, I knew part of that was because she hadn't fawned over me, because she'd called me on my shit during a time in my life when women had been common and frequent and accommodating. But not Olivia. *Never* Olivia.

We were all business, and so I'd tucked the attraction away.

Now it was out, and I didn't know how to put it back.

I tucked the pillow against a rock, pulled the jacket on over my damp shirt, and lay down, tossing the blanket over me. It was thin as hell and just reinforced the fact that it was going to be a bitterly cold night.

In the meantime, I tried to puzzle out what I'd discovered.

Absolutely no use of the nickname Vivie. Viv seemed fine, though I wasn't sure if it would be fine coming from me. That was the critical question, it seemed. Was it me? Or was it the name? But she'd come out to see me, to pass on news that wasn't critical, and I didn't think she would do that with another client . . . or maybe that was just ego talking.

"Fuck," I muttered, knowing that I would probably never understand Olivia unless she decided to let me in. And since that seemed about as likely to happen as hell becoming my own personal ice rink, I just had to deal with not understanding her reaction.

Seeing as the sun was fully down and I was exhausted after my rescuing, I decided this was as good a time as any to go to sleep. Stifling another sigh because the last thing I needed to do was to resemble a hormonal teenager, I settled against the pillow and tried to ignore the fact that it was uncomfortable as hell and my back wasn't what it once was. I'd played ten seasons of professional hockey, not to mention the ten previous as I'd made my way up through the amateur ranks. Which meant I'd dealt with my share of injuries. It also meant that my body wasn't what it used to be, and I wasn't looking forward to how it would feel waking up in the morning.

Bucky chuffed and I listened to him settling in, letting the sound of the waves crashing wash over me, drawing me closer to sleep. Odd twist of events or not, I still found my peace, just like every other time I was out here.

I let my eyes slide closed.

Blackness swept me under.

THE CRACK of a twig snapping nearby brought me to rigid attention.

My lids flew open and I blinked, trying to adjust my vision to the darkness.

Another *snap*.

Then a curse.

A feminine curse that belonged to a sexy female whose voice I knew almost better than my own.

Rolling quietly to my side, I watched her make her way through the trees and rocks, hobbling across the rough ground, the socks not doing much to help protect her feet.

"Fuck, fuckity, fuck, *fuck*," she muttered, picking her way across to the tent.

I didn't say a word, which I knew was decidedly in the

realm of creepy, but I couldn't find it in myself to care, not when I had the chance to observe her in an unguarded moment.

Even in the bulky clothes, she was still the most attractive woman I'd ever laid eyes on. Curvy, confident in her body, in her femininity. I might not be the guy who loved to get into a suit and tie—I'd had more than enough of that during my playing days—but I'd always loved the way she dressed. Tight slacks, high heels, blouses that seemed destined to drive me crazy.

I'd nix the heels while beachcombing if it were up to me, but since I didn't purport to think I had a single say in what Olivia wore—

"*Fuck,*" she hissed, jumping on one foot while holding the other.

Which lasted all of a few seconds before she tipped to the side. I was on my feet before my brain processed the movement, arms wrapping around her waist, catching her against my chest.

Curves.

All those fucking luscious curves pressed to me.

Her breath caught, spine stiffening as I lifted her off her feet and carried her to the tent. All along the way, her scent filled my nose—flowers mixed with salt—and it took everything in me to not bury my face in her hair and inhale.

"What—"

I bent and deposited her on the sleeping bag, nudging the unzipped flap of the tent to the side as I did so.

"Cole   "

Ignoring her, I leaned back on my heels and picked up her foot. I got the sock off then used the flashlight from my pack to examine the bare skin. Blood dripped from a cut just beneath her toes.

Fucking hell.

"It's—"

I reached for my pack again and extracted the first aid kit and a bottle of water, using the latter to rinse the cut and the former to clean, dry, and bandage the injury. "No walking," I ordered, unrolling the too-long leg of the sweats I'd loaned her down and over her foot so it wouldn't be cold.

"I'm—"

I narrowed my eyes. "No walking, and definitely no fucking heels."

She huffed, yanking her foot from my grasp. "It's a fucking cut. That's it. And less than half an inch at that."

"It's dirty out here," I said through gritted teeth.

"*I'm fine,*" she replied through some gritting of her own.

"Infection can set in—"

"Oh, for fuck's sake," she said, flopping back onto the sleeping bag and glancing up at the top of the tent. "I seem to remember you having your own cuts and staying on the ice with them bleeding down your face."

This woman was beyond the pale.

"I had several trainers and a team doctor to look after me," I said, sweeping an arm out to the trees and dirt surrounding them. "Don't see any of them here, do you?"

"No, but I'm fine because you treated a tiny cut like you were proceeding over an open-heart operation."

"Because it's dirty and infection—"

She kept her eyes on the roof of the tent. "Heaven save me from mansplaining men. I understand how infection works. I also think that I could have *walked* over to the tent, poured some water on the cut, slapped a Band-Aid over it, and *still* have kept my foot."

"You—"

She slapped her hands on the sleeping bag then pushed up to sitting. "You know what? I'm done." Olivia shoved past me, hair whipping across my cheek as she crammed herself through the opening of the tent and onto her feet.

It was the wavering that did it.

Well, that and the way she favored her foot.

Or maybe the fact that she picked up her heels and seemed to be contemplating putting them back on.

I grabbed her arm. "Don't you *fucking* dare."

She yanked it free. "I will *fucking* dare," she snapped. "I will do whatever the fuck, whenever the fuck, *however* the fuck I want." She stepped closer, her mouth mere centimeters from his, so close that he felt the heat of her breath against his lips. "So, fuck you, Cole," she said. "Just because you saved me from drowning—and thank you for that—but it also doesn't mean you can control what I do."

"I'm not trying to control you, dammit." I dropped my hands to her shoulders. "I respect you so fucking much, Olivia. You're brilliant. You're the reason I could afford to have this property and do what I'm doing with the ranch in the first place." I stared into her eyes, willing her to understand. "But like it or not, we both know each other. Extremely well. And I know you'd rather cut off your own leg than accept help."

"I—"

"No bullshit now." I released her, stepped back, and took her shoes from her hands and launched them across the clearing.

"Cole! What the fuck?"

"I'll get you to your car in the morning," I told her. "I'll get you home when it's safe, but now is not the time."

Silence.

Long, drawn-out silence with both of our breaths slowing.

Lengthening quiet as we looked at each other and then our breathing began speeding up again.

She took a hobbling step toward me. Another. And another .

. . until she was pressed to me, until I could feel those rapid inhalations and exhalations against my chest, the soft of her brushing along the hard of me. The full length of her rubbed along my front, the flowers and salt scent of her surrounding me. She rose on tiptoe, lips parting, and—

Winced.

I didn't think. Just reacted.

One moment she was pressed to me, the next she was in my arms, all of those soft curves protected in my hold.

I'd intended to put her back on the sleeping bag, to set her safely inside the tent . . . and maybe guard the opening so she couldn't escape until morning.

But then one of her hands found my cheek, cupping it gently.

Her lips pressed to mine, tongue sliding across the seam of my mouth.

Then her other hand slipped between our bodies and drifted down my stomach.

SEVEN

Olivia

ONE SECOND, I was in his arms, floating through the air. The next, I was on the ground, the hard surface slightly muted by the padding of the sleeping bag, but that wasn't the hard I was focused on.

Nope, the *hard* on top of me, pressing me down into the slippery material of the sleeping bag was much more interesting.

Cole's mouth hadn't left mine, and it was everything I'd ever dreamed it could be. He had the best lips of any man I'd ever seen, so soft and lush they should have looked ridiculous on his gorgeous face. Instead, they managed to temper the rugged lines of his jaw and nose, make the scars from playing such a physical sport fade away.

All that was left was Cole.

Lovely, kind Cole.

My stomach twisted and I turned away, feeling bile burn the back of my throat. This man was—*had been*—a client, but more than that, he was just so fucking nice.

And I'd slapped him.

He'd bandaged my foot, and I'd yelled at him.

He'd saved me from drowning, and I'd—

I swallowed hard, turning my head to the side, and blinking rapidly. Fuck, I was such a mess. I'd thought I'd gotten over my childhood, had proved myself better than my mother, better than the shithole I'd grown up in.

And I'd slapped him. Yelled at him. Invaded his peace.

"Honey."

I swallowed again.

I'd done all those things to Cole, but I sure as fuck wasn't going to puke on him.

"I can't do this," I said, hating the way my voice sounded— weak, broken, sad, so much unlike me. I put my hands to his chest and shoved.

To Cole's credit, he immediately leaned back, shifting to the side. But the tent was small, and he couldn't go far. "Did I hurt you?" he asked.

"No."

I'd done that myself.

He seemed to understand what I was thinking, his tone beyond soft now. "Honey."

"I need to go."

"It's pitch black, and we're on a cliff. I don't know what's happening here, Olivia, but you trying to sprint off when it's too dangerous to run miles through the woods isn't the smart, capable woman I know," he said quietly. "I'm worried you hit your head."

For some reason, that made me laugh.

Not because I had a brain injury, I hadn't been lying before. I'd been pressed to the sand, waves crashing over me, but I hadn't hit my head against the rocks. I wasn't dizzy or disoriented, didn't have any concussion symptoms.

Instead, my past had escaped the locked box I'd spent a lifetime keeping it confined in.

In front of Cole.

The one man I'd always liked and respected, the one I'd always wanted but couldn't have.

The one man I'd tried to consistently have my shit together for.

And tonight, I'd lost it.

Twice.

I stared at the mesh at the top of the tent. "I didn't hit my head."

"Then what?"

A sigh before I admitted, "You're a good person."

Silence.

Then, "Is the implication of that statement that *you're* not?"

"I think that's obvious."

More silence, long enough that my pulse had slowed and, somehow, my lids were drifting closed. Maybe it was the drive up, followed by the near-drowning, and the lashing whip of my memories. But I thought it was more likely that it was just Cole and the warmth of his body, nearby but not touching, the spicy male scent of him clouding the air that had me relaxing back into the sleeping bag.

He was quiet for ages before he rolled over. I felt his eyes on me but kept my own closed, my breathing slow and steady.

Maybe he'd think I was asleep and then I could just slip out and—

What?

Wander alone through the wilderness in a pair of socks, with no phone and no sense of where I was going? It wasn't like I could use the stars to navigate, and even if I could, the fog had come in, blurring the landscape around us.

I hadn't even been able to make it safely to and from the bush I'd used as a bathroom without hurting myself.

With my luck that day, I'd fall off the cliff.

"I've always thought you were the most beautiful woman I've ever seen."

He'd realized I wasn't asleep.

That probably shouldn't have been the first thought that went through my mind, but then again, my eyes had flown open at his gentle tone, locked on the roof of the tent. Or maybe that was because he'd brushed his finger down my nose.

"I swear to God," he continued, murmuring. "I've had more fantasies about you over the years we've known each other than when I was a teenager."

I found I couldn't stop myself from rolling to face him. "You were practically a teenager when we met."

"And you were an intern." A flash of white in the dark light. "And *this* teenager's wet dream."

That made me blush. It shouldn't have. I felt like I had spent most of my formative years in locker rooms and around much dirtier sentiments. I considered myself unblushable, completely unflappable. Hell, I'd seen more penises in my lifetime than a porn star.

And yet, Cole.

Or rather, thinking about Cole hard and aching, turned on by his fantasies of me, *that* made me blush.

It also made my filter disappear.

"I've thought of you, too."

He went stiff. "You—" He shifted closer, the inches separating us becoming centimeters, then less as his front pressed to my side. "You've thought of me?"

My teeth sank into my bottom lip as I considered what I had admitted. Then, maybe it was the fog or the waves crashing in the background, perhaps it was Cole's scent in my nose and the heat of his body against my side. Whatever it was, I decided that I didn't have anything to lose in that moment, and so I rolled to my side to face him.

"Yes."

His eyes were black in the dim light, but I watched them get even darker at my admission. "Honey?"

"Yeah?"

"*You've* thought about me?"

It was hard to shrug when I was on my side, but I managed it, at least one shoulder.

"A lot?"

Another one of those awkward shrugs.

His hand lifted, resting on my hip, and I swear to everything that was holy—which for me was namely Louboutins and sparkly Kate Spade purses—that I felt the heat of his hand like it was on my bare skin, and not through the thick layer of cotton. "For how long?"

I swallowed. "A while."

Fingers squeezing lightly. "How long?"

"Long enough."

His hand rose again and before I had a chance to miss it, he moved it up, used his palm to cup my cheek. Heat. Breath catching. Rough against smooth. "How long?"

I shook my head, feeling my hair slide over his skin. "I said, it doesn't matter."

He chuckled, and I felt it arrow between my thighs. "Always so stubborn," he said, and his palm peeled up, though his fingers stayed in place, and the calloused ends raised goose bumps on my arms when he stroked them along my jaw.

"There's a reason that people call me a bitch."

Suddenly, I found myself on my back, Cole on top of me, and it was fucking glorious, but more glorious were his words, his flashing eyes, the tightness in his jaw.

Not directed at me. Instead he was frustrated *for* me.

"That's fucking bullshit, and you know it. Only tiny-dicked little assholes would call you a bitch," he growled. "You say it how it is. That's a good thing. I *always* know where I stand with you. That's a *really* good thing. So no, fuck whoever says that. *They're* the bitches."

"I—"

I opened and closed my mouth a few times, trying to process the words, trying to understand why hearing something I'd told myself a million times spoken aloud hit me so hard.

Then I shook my head, not because I didn't believe the words, but because thus was the power of Cole.

I respected him, valued his opinion.

That was why I tucked the sentiment close.

What I didn't anticipate was Cole's reaction to my headshake.

"Honey," he murmured, cupping my jaw again for a brief moment before flipping us, so I was cradled against his chest. "How do you not see yourself clearly?"

I saw myself *very* clearly.

That was the problem.

But I also really liked the way he was holding me, the gentleness with how I was cuddled against him, the warmth and scent and comfort seeping into me.

Still, I was me, and me being *me* meant that I couldn't just lie there and let him hold and comfort me, not without him understanding the monster he was cradling so carefully in his arms.

Yes, I was being dramatic.

No, that wasn't going to stop me.

"I know myself," I said. "And one of the things that I know down to the marrow in my bones is that I will never be the kind of woman a man wants long term. I know I'm smart and pretty,"

I hurried to add when I felt the protest bubbling up in his chest. "I know I'm capable and fuckable and tough. But"—and here was the truth that I didn't want to give, but knew I had to anyway—"I'm not a girl who will ever be content to be in a relationship like the one you want. I've been clawing my way out of my shitty childhood for most of my life, and that's left scars." My voice dropped. "And on top of those scars, armor. Heavy, impenetrable armor that no one will ever be able to penetrate. I'm not that woman, Cole. Not the kind, sweet one you'll want to make a life with, and it's time we both stop thinking about each other and move on to what we deserve."

Work for me.

A family and fulfilling life for him.

Quiet, but when I lifted my gaze to meet his again, I didn't see what I expected. Instead of distance, there was understanding.

I felt a blip of alarm in knowing that I'd given Cole understanding.

I'd been trying to insert distance and—

"How do you know what kind of relationship I want?"

I blinked, that having been pretty much the last response I'd expected to my droning. "Um—"

"I've had sweet and kind," he said. "It's fucking boring. I like fire, honey. I like to bicker over whether my woman should wear heels in a fucking forest and to argue whether I should model for an underwear line—hint: no fucking way. I like a challenge. I like strong. I like a woman who tells it how it is."

My heart rate had picked up, and it felt as though the organ would pound out of my chest. "You say that now."

His forehead pressed to mine. "I say that after having known you for more than a decade. I say that after having seen you grow from promising intern into a fabulous and capable agent who oversaw my career for eight years. I say that after having seen your temper flare more than once and cheering you on when you stood up for yourself." A kiss to the tip of my nose. "I know you, Olivia."

"Then you know I'm a pain in the ass."

A flash of white. "You're fucking incredible."

"Zero stars. Would not recommend."

He snorted. "Strong. Tough. Spine of steel."

"I don't let people slide when they're wrong."

"I don't need someone to excuse my bad behavior." He touched his lips to my cheek. "And I've never seen you shy away from someone correcting *you* either."

Maybe that was true. It stung when I was wrong, but I'd preferred someone to tell me rather than stumbling around like an uninformed idiot.

"I work a lot."

"So do I." A shrug. "I also don't need a babysitter."

"I'm not the type of woman who'll have dinner on the table when you walk through the door."

His tongue touched the corner of my mouth, and my breath caught. "I can cook."

It was his tongue, that flick of hot and wet against my skin, that made me blurt, "My mother called me Vivie, and things weren't . . . good."

He sucked in a breath. "Then it's Olivia from here on out."

Silence then, "I'll probably never open up."

That one gave him pause. Then, "Not sure what you think opening up is, honey."

"What?"

"You gave me that tonight."

I frowned. "I hardly gave you anything."

His mouth curved. "Then I can't wait to hear the rest of it, whenever and however you're comfortable. You decide when you're ready to drop that armor around me, I'll catch it and hang it on the wall so that it's ready for you to don when you head back in the world." His lips on my cheek, my jaw, my ear. "You eventually decide that I'm safe enough to be around without that, I'll never underestimate how much that cost you." His voice rasped along my throat. "Because I know you, Olivia."

I opened my mouth to say . . .

Fuck if I knew.

It felt as though someone had taken my world and spun it in the opposite direction, realigning its axis and sending me for a loop.

"Now," he murmured, shifting to the side, zipping up the tent, then flicking the opening of the sleeping bag over us. "Stop talking and sleep."

And somehow—maybe because of that world shifting, or more likely because Cole had ordered it and he was warm and holding me tightly against him—I managed to shut my mouth.

A moment later, I managed to shut my eyes.

And a moment after that, I tipped headlong into sleep.

EIGHT

Cole

I LAY awake for a long time, just enjoying the feel of Olivia in my arms.

Right.

This was absolutely right.

She'd given me a lot before she'd succumbed to exhaustion, even thinking she hadn't, and I turned the pieces over in my mind, knowing there was still a lot for me to learn hiding under that armor. I'd been given a sliver, and I needed to decide that night if I was going to dive in there, make that sliver something larger, something I could make myself at home in.

Because I knew if I did, there was no going back.

I wasn't the type of man to force my way into a woman's heart and then leave.

I lived in commitments and permanents, and Olivia deserved to have a man who knew everything about her and loved her all the more for it. I thought I could be that man, but I needed to be absolutely sure.

Could I handle the battle, the struggle she was sure to give me on the way?

Could I get her to trust me?

Could I put myself out there, knowing I may not ever get the equal in return? And if that happened, never getting fully into Olivia's heart, would that be enough?

I thought myself in circles, understanding that mentally I was standing outside on the cliffside, readying myself to take a leap. Then I realized I would *always* leap.

For Olivia, it was never a question.

That cliff was no barrier.

It had *always* been her.

And so, decision made, I watched the sky get brighter, black turning into navy, the fog slowly burning off, becoming progressively brighter, hints of orange and pink and red transforming into a pale blue that was very close to Olivia's eyes.

Seeing her eyes in the sky was the last piece.

I'd been seeing her everywhere in my life since the moment I'd laid eyes on her, the red of her lips was the color of my truck, her shining black hair the Tesla I'd recently ordered. I heard her laugh in my sleep, smelled her scent in the flowers when out riding. She was everywhere and—

She was mine.

Now, to convince her of that.

OLIVIA WAS on Bucky's back and looking ridiculously adorable.

Not that I was going to tell her that.

Her scowl was fierce, her nose wrinkled, her blue eyes shooting fire at me. Probably because I'd cut off her argument about not riding my horse by picking her up and depositing her into the saddle. Though, she hadn't attempted to slide down, like I'd thought she would, and had instead picked up the reins like she'd done the same thing a hundred times before.

"You better have packed up my heels carefully."

I'd grinned, since they were already securely stored in Buck's pack, then had patted my horse on the rump and moved to his shoulder to lead him to the proper trail—that being the one that would lead us to Olivia's car, rather than the one that led back to the ranch.

"I could have walked," she muttered, when I slipped the reins from her hands, not because she didn't look comfortable on the back of the horse, but because it gave me a reason to stick close.

"You *could* have," I said, leaving off the part where that would have happened over my dead body, and asking her instead, "How'd you learn to ride?"

She went stiff, and I thought for sure she wouldn't answer.

Then, as Olivia was wont to do, she surprised me.

"I grew up in a saddle."

I know my eyes were wide when I glanced up at her, but because they were, I didn't miss the smirk curving her lips. "This girly girl surprised you?"

"You're full of surprises, honey."

That made the curve disappear, but because her expression softened, I didn't worry when her words snapped through the air between us. "Damn right, McTavish."

"I didn't learn until I was an adult," I said.

Her brows drew down. "But you've had horses for as long as I've known you."

I shrugged. "Most professional athletes buy a car or a house with their first big paycheck. I bought a horse."

She snorted.

"Hey," I said, knowing she was teasing. "She was both a companion *and* transportation."

More curving of her mouth, but this time it was a grin. "I can just see you riding up to the rink, your hockey stick slung over your back."

"Luckily, I had good equipment managers."

She laughed. "And a stable, I'm guessing."

I nodded. "That, and a really shitty car for a couple of years to pay for that and a condo."

"I'm guessing the horse and her care was more expensive than the apartment."

"Maybe."

She laughed again, and the tinkling sound slid down my spine. I watched it have the same effect on Bucky as well, my horse absorbing the cheerful noise, his flanks tensing then relaxing as a chuff slid out his nostrils.

Buck liked her.

Never let it be said my horse didn't have good taste.

Absently, Olivia ran a hand along Buck's neck, the bright red of her fingernails in sharp contrast to the fawn-colored hair.

And now I was jealous of my pet.

"So, why'd you buy a horse?"

I guided Bucky around a tree and down a slight incline. "I got Bessie because she was a retired racehorse."

"Must not have been much of one." I glanced up at her and raised a brow. "Bessie isn't exactly a name for a famous racehorse."

"Oh," I said. "Well, her official name was Bessahima Prometheus Augustina the Second."

"There was a *first?*"

I chuckled. "Apparently. So, for obvious reasons, I called her Bessie."

"Where did you keep her?"

"A ranch outside of L.A."—I'd played my first few seasons

for the Kings—"She was happy for quite a few years before I had to put her down."

Hardest thing I'd ever done to date, holding the blanket over Bessie's eyes as the vet had sedated then euthanized her. But she'd barely been able to walk at that point, her joints so painful that I'd known I couldn't selfishly keep her with me any longer.

A hand on my shoulder. "I'm sorry," she murmured.

Just two words, but I knew she got it, knew she'd been through something similar, but before I could ask, she volunteered the information. And I knew that I'd made the right decision in the dark hours of that morning, knew that I was in this, knew I wouldn't give up on Olivia.

"My horse was Butterfly." A flash of white. "I guess we like the B names."

"Not gonna touch that with a ten-foot pole."

"What—? *Oh*." Her eyes narrowed, and she smacked me lightly. "Not *that* B name, though we both know I think bitch isn't an insult."

"I—"

"Shush, you. I'm trying to tell you about Butterfly." She patted Bucky's neck again. "He was about Bucky's color—"

"*He?*"

"Yes, he," she said. "There are male butterflies, you know. And also, I got him when I was six. My world was butterflies and unicorns and—" She broke off, smile fading. "Anyway, I was every girly stereotype reduced down into a tiny thirty-something-pound six-year-old explosion of pink and purple and sparkles. And I wanted nothing more in the world than a unicorn."

I chuckled.

"Yeah," she said. "Exactly. But the next best thing aside from mythical creatures was a horse."

When she was quiet for a minute or two, I asked, "Then came Butterfly?"

Her eyes had been on the ocean in the distance. "Yeah. My dad bought him for me. I loved him, soaked up every bit of information he gave me for his care, loved brushing his tail—he even let me braid ribbons into it." She turned and smiled, but I knew the sad was coming, could see it edging into her expression. "Then we had to sell him."

My heart squeezed. "Oliv—"

She shrugged. "It wasn't a big deal. I mean, it *was* a big deal. I was only eight and I'd had him for two years, which felt like my entire life, but it wasn't like my dad had a choice. It was either he went, or we didn't eat."

I sucked in a breath.

"It was rough, no lie, but it was also just a lesson in how life is sometimes." Another shrug. "Things get tough. We sacrifice."

"I don't think any eight-year-old should have to learn that particular life lesson."

Her hand went to my shoulder again, squeezed lightly. "That's why you're a good person, Cole."

There she went again, calling me good when I could tell by her tone that she equated my being good with her being *not* good, as though I was simply a better person, no matter the circumstances of our upbringings or the decisions we'd both made in our lives.

It was total bullshit.

But I knew that I wouldn't be able to convince her differently in that moment.

I was going to have to show her, and that was going to take time.

I didn't know how a woman who burned so brightly in life, who was so smart and beautiful and funny, who managed to give the impression of living fully and totally out there could have pulled the wool over everyone's eyes—including mine—for so long. I'd seen the distance there, of course, but I'd internalized it as me because . . .

Why?

Oh.

Because she'd wielded that distance with charm and a sharp wit.

Calling me on my shit while pretending to be self-deprecating, all so she could prove to the world she could handle dishing it out *and* taking it.

But it wasn't self-deprecating so much as self-loathing.

And that worried me.

Still, we were in the middle of nowhere, walking along a trail that was skirting the ocean. The sun was shining bright, the salty tang of the sea breeze coating the air.

We'd had enough heavy.

I hoped I could prove to Olivia that what she was inside was just as good as her outside, but I also knew that ultimately, it had to come from her.

So, I tucked away the heavy, pushed down the sad memories, and I asked her about movies.

Which got us into a debate about which *Die Hard* was the best—the first obviously, though for some crazy reason, she thought the third—but it also got her smiling and joking and laughing.

And for that moment, it was enough.

NINE

Olivia

MY CAR WAS DEAD.

Dead enough that Cole couldn't make it work, and he seemed to know what he was doing, banging around under the hood.

Heh.

I'd like him to bang around under *my* hood.

Which was most of the problem.

Of course, I was semi-delirious, rubbed raw from the inside out. Part of it was sleeping in the tent, riding on top of the horse, being out in nature. The rest was all Cole and the way he'd held me, as though I were fragile and valuable, the way he'd talked to me, kind and encouraging, the way he looked at me, intense but gentle.

Bucky grazed nearby. We'd put him in the small pasture next to the rundown barn, its fence intact enough that he wouldn't wander off without us.

Not that it was a big worry.

He was a good horse.

My car, on the other hand, wasn't good.

It was a temperamental pain in the ass.

Cole poked his head out from around the hood and sighed before walking over and leaning back against the car next to me. I'd sprawled there, enjoying the warm metal against my spine and trying to pretend that my thighs being sore after riding Bucky for a little over an hour wasn't a comfort. That wasn't an oxymoron, wasn't it?

The slight twinge of my thigh muscles shouldn't be a good thing.

But it was.

The rustling of Bucky's mane, the *clip-clop* of his hooves on the ground, his chuffs and snorts shouldn't be sounds that I found comforting.

But they were.

And so I was stuck firmly in the past when Cole leaned next to me and said, "I don't know anything about cars."

My spine went straight. "What?"

He gave me a sheepish grin. "I don't know what the hell I'm doing under there."

That had better be a reference to my car and not messing around under *my* hood. I had high hopes that he knew what he was doing under *there* and—

Focus.

And not on how cute he looked smiling down at me, all hangdog.

"What were you doing then?"

He shrugged. "Banging around on a few things, pretending I knew what I was looking for."

I shook my head, surprised that he would admit to not knowing something when most of the men I'd known would die a slow, agonizing death before doing so. "You didn't break anything, did you?"

"I don't think so."

"Think?" I raised a brow.

"No," he said. "I didn't. Mostly, I was checking to make sure the battery cables were attached and looked okay."

My other brow lifted. "Seriously?"

"It's the only trick I know."

I sighed. "Okay. So now what?"

"We'll ride to the ranch," he said. "Need anything from the car before we go?"

"What could I possibly need?" I asked.

Pink crept onto the corners of his cheeks. "You're Ms. Prepared. Don't you carry a change of clothes or something? Extra shoes?"

That I couldn't deny. I did carry emergency supplies, but since those spare shoes were actually heels and the spare clothes in my trunk were another pair of slacks and a silk blouse, they wouldn't exactly be the best option for extended time on horseback. The underwear and bra *would* be however, so I used my key to manually unlock the trunk.

Turned out a key fob meeting saltwater had fared about as well as the cell phone.

"It feels weird to be without my cell for so long," I muttered, scrounging through the bag and trying to pocket the bra and underwear surreptitiously.

"Disconnecting is a good thing," he said.

"Yeah," I replied. "So says the retired old man."

He snorted. "I believe we're only a couple of months apart, and since I'm thirty-two, that means you're . . ."

"I stopped aging at twenty-nine, actually," I said, zipping up the bag and closing the trunk. "It's a fact of nature. Women just stop getting older at twenty-nine."

Lips twitching, he murmured, "Funny that."

"Yup. *So* funny." I began to limp my way back over to Bucky, trying to hide my discomfort with every step. It wasn't the most painful injury I'd ever had—that had occurred at the age of thirteen when I'd slipped down a leafy hillside and toppled into a ravine. I still remembered the way the rocks had felt as they'd cut into the skin of my back, tearing through my shirt, and how bruised and battered I'd been the next day from the fall.

This was nothing like that.

This was a sore foot and a stiff back from sleeping on the ground.

I was totally fine—

"*Ack!*"

Not a graceful sound, but also the way that Cole scooped me up and tossed me over his shoulder was nothing approximating graceful. It was surprising. It stole all the air from my lungs, and it—

Well, hey now, I had a very nice view of his ass.

Hockey players had the best asses.

Round and firm and totally cup-able.

"Stop looking at my butt, sweetheart," he said, clamping his hand over the back of my knees to stop me from squirming free.

"First," I said, unabashedly watching that butt move as he strode through the dry grass toward Bucky, "I physically cannot *not* look at your ass because it's right in my face. And second—"

My breath caught when his other hand cupped *my* ass.

"Second, what?" he asked, voice husky.

His palm was hot through the sweatpants, and I was suddenly *very* aware of the fact that I wasn't wearing underwear . . . and also that the pants were drawstring.

It would take hardly anything for him to be inside me.

Drop me to the ground. Untie the sweats. Push them down and—

"Second, I'm not wearing any underwear."

Fuck. *Shit.* That hadn't been what I was planning on saying. My second point was supposed to have been that I was fully capable of walking over to Bucky and that I didn't need a man to carry me and—

I was on my feet before I finished my thought of second points, Cole's brown eyes molten and locked on me, his large palms spanning my hips.

"Olivia."

I bit my lip, saw those eyes heat further, then immediately released it. "I didn't mean to say that."

A curve of his mouth, those fingers on my hips convulsing. "Maybe not, but fuck, honey. You're killing me all the same."

My gaze drifted down.

It shouldn't have.

All the reasons I'd had for not getting involved with him still existed. I was just having a hard time remembering why they were deterrents rather than reasons to launch myself into his arms and kiss him senseless.

That was why my eyes slid toward his pelvis, why the sight of him hard and pressing against his jeans nearly made my knees buckle—

Why I forgot all of my deterrents and launched myself into his arms.

My mouth hit his and, *fuck*, was it perfect. Soft lips, probing tongue, hot mouth. His hands shifted from having caught me around the waist, to banding tight around my back, yanking me against the hard muscles of his thighs and chest. He tasted of mint and cinnamon, the hint of a morning toothbrushing trailed by his preferred cinnamon chewing gum, and it was like coming home, that spice against my tongue. Heat engulfed me from head to toe, burning along my nerve endings, soaking into my stomach, between my thighs, making my nipples pebble into tight hot buds.

Then my knees actually did buckle, but Cole was there, catching me before I collapsed and tucking me tighter against him as we kissed and kissed and kissed.

His palm slipped under my sweatshirt, the slightly rough surface almost scalding as it brushed up and down my back, sliding up between my shoulder blades then down to dip under the loose waistband of the sweats.

Tease.

I reached between us and undid the tie.

The fabric puddled at my ankles.

"Olivia—"

I wasn't completely exposed since his sweatshirt was big and covered me down to mid-thigh, but the sudden wash of cold air over my heated skin was enough for a full-bodied shiver to pass through me.

Cole cursed and my eyes jumped to his. "Killing. Me," he muttered.

Since dropping my pants pretty much meant I'd blown off any potential consequences of me pursuing something with him, I'd decided to forgo my fears and. Just. Keep. Leaping.

"Well," I said, widening my legs. "I was actually hoping you'd eat *me*."

I'd barely gotten the words out of my mouth before he was on me, fingers spreading me wide, lips latching onto my clit. I'd expected him to tackle me to the dry-grass covered ground, to feel the prickles of the weeds and rocks against my back and thighs. What I *didn't* expect was for his mouth to be between my thighs, his free arm clamping around my waist and keeping me pressed to his face as he fell to his back.

My knees hit the dirt, and I felt a slight sting, but it hardly processed because then both of his hands had found my thighs and spread me wide while I sat on his mouth.

In the middle of a field.

In the middle of the day.

But fuck if I was thinking about any of that.

Instead, my focus was on his tongue flicking against my clit, finding a pattern that sent me soaring in seconds, pleasure spinning out from my center and filling my limbs with heat. Those hands coaxed me forward, my palms hitting the dirt by his head as he drove his tongue inside me. One palm slid up the inside of my sweatshirt, cupping my breast, then pinching my nipple just on the right side of rough. The other slipped in, taking over the rhythm of his tongue and alternately circling and tapping my clit.

Hot. Wet. Pleasure spiraling up and up until . . .

"Fuck!" I cried. "Cole. Oh God. Don't fucking stop."

He groaned and the sound vibrated through me, catapulting me over the edge.

I rode his mouth through the orgasm, not giving two fucks that it was still the middle of the day and we were still completely out in the open. If anything, with the fear of getting caught like this prickling the back of my mind, worry that someone might see me straddling his face and coming all over him had made the entire thing the hottest experience of my life.

But more than that, this was about Cole and me, about the way he made me feel and the fucking incredibleness of his tongue.

I'd known it would be good between us . . . or at least I'd hoped that would be the case, just based on the sheer volume of attraction I felt for him. To have this proof, to be able to come this fast in this risky of a place . . . yeah, Cole and I had it going on, at least between the sheets—*cough*—dried blades of grass? Rotting fence posts?

His tongue flicked out and brushed my clit, making me jump and focus back on the man between my thighs.

I was probably smothering the poor guy.

But when I went to move back, to allow him some undoubtedly much-needed oxygen, his hand slid around my hips and held me close.

Then he nuzzled me, lips moving across my labia, causing heat to prickle outward again, my pelvis to tilt forward and seek the pleasure it knew it could find from that beautiful mouth. I could tell he was smiling, knew it would be cocky—

Which reminded me.

I wanted something else that was along that variety.

Sliding backward, I moved down his chest, straddling his waist as I leaned forward to nip at his lips. I got a taste of myself mingled with mint and cinnamon for my trouble, and it was fucking hot, those flavors bursting to life on my tongue. But while kissing Cole was incredible, I wanted more.

And that more was going to be in the form of his hard cock in my mouth.

Then in my pussy.

I flicked open the button on his jeans.

Fingers laced with mine, staying me from lowering the zipper. I glared up at him. "If this is your play to make some noble bullshit move to protect my feelings in order to stop me from getting my mouth on you, you're a fucking idiot," I snapped. "I'm a big girl, Cole, and I want to suck your cock."

His hips lurched up. "Not trying to stop you from putting your mouth on me, honey," he said. "But I figured you need to know the bad news that I don't have a condom before we go any further."

Oh.

Oh.

I grinned as I batted his hands away. "I've got good news, baby." An alarm blared in the deepest recesses of my mind, knowing I'd never used an endearment like that with a man before, knowing that the fact I had with Cole was important, that this thing with him was more important than me just telling myself I'd finally taken the plunge and explored my long-held attraction.

It was more than sexual chemistry.

But luckily in that moment, my conscious mind was on the back burner, and my more primitive one was in control.

I freed his cock from his boxer briefs and wrapped my hand around the hard length of him. Then I bent and ran my tongue from base to tip, loving the way he got harder, the litany of harsh curses that were torn out of his mouth. "I'm on the birth control implant," I murmured before sucking him in deep.

He groaned, hips shooting up again. "Don't know what that means."

"It means"—I took him deep again then released him with a soft *pop*—"that I can't get pregnant for three years after having it."

"Please, tell me you're within those three years."

I swirled my tongue around the head. "Yup. And I'm clean, baby. Just got tested and haven't slept with anyone else in months." I blew out a breath, letting my lips brush the tip of him, teasing him by letting him in just the slightest bit.

Cole's hands tangled in my hair, tugging me off his cock, and the restraint I felt in the way he held me still even though I could tell he wanted to yank my head up and down his cock, had my thighs squeezing together. "Never slept with anyone without a condom, honey. Not once." My breath caught, my heart leaping with joy that I was about to give him something he'd never had before. "And I was tested six months ago. Haven't been with anyone since."

"Good," I said, my lips curved. "Now, can I get back to sucking your cock?"

His fingers clenched in my hair for a millisecond before relaxing down to his sides. "Far be it for me to stop a woman from doing what she wants."

I chuckled. "Right answer."

And then I parted my lips and let him slide deep into my mouth.

Thick, was my first thought, quickly followed by rock-hard and long. But then my mind focused less on the tangible and more on the desire to make Cole's experience as incredible as the one he'd given me. I pulled out every trick I'd learned over the years, using my mouth and hands in tandem, relaxing my throat so I could get all of him inside, cupping his balls, stroking the length of him, generally driving him insane as I brought him up to the edge.

I would have brought him over that edge, too, condom and health talk or not. The feel of him in my mouth, the way he groaned my name, how his fingers were clenching and unclenching at his sides . . . all of that meant that I was dripping wet, more turned on than I'd ever been in my life, and wanting nothing more than to feel him come apart between my lips.

"No," he rasped, tugging my head from his cock and hauling me up so I was sprawled against his chest.

I barely had time to suck in a breath before his mouth was against mine and his cock was sinking inside me. Fuck, he was big, or maybe he was just as turned on as me, harder than normal, thicker than normal, especially when pressing against my hot and swollen tissues.

Either way it took my breath away, having him inside me.

He seemed to feel the same way because he paused, chest

rising and falling in rapid succession, his forehead glinting with sweat, his eyes so fucking intense as they met mine that I had to pause and just breathe, palm bracing myself upright on his chest.

Then his mouth turned up and his hands dropped to my thighs. "Move, honey."

I didn't need to be told twice.

My rhythm was hard and fast and a little rough, but Cole was right there with me, slipping one hand down and using his thumb to circle my clit, the other still on my hip, coaxing me to move faster, harder, *rougher*.

And all the while he encouraged me on, telling me how beautiful I was, how good my hot pussy felt as it clamped down on him, how much he'd wanted me.

"Come on me, honey," he murmured. "Let me feel how tight that pussy can get around me. Let me feel you come." His thumb pressed hard, and I toppled over the edge, limbs going limp as my orgasm tore through me. I barely managed to stay upright as he kept thrusting in to me, prolonging my pleasure, before giving into his own with a low groan.

I gave up my fight with staying upright and collapsed against his chest.

Cole's arms wrapped me tight, one on my ass, the other around my shoulders, as we lay pressed together, pulses slowly returning to normal. I expected to want to disengage, to back away and get dressed and get out, just like every other time I'd slept with a man.

This was different.

I didn't care that I was sweaty in the layers covering my top half, nor did I give two shits that my ass was hanging out in the open.

I was with Cole.

Me. With Cole.

That was the thought that finally snapped me back to reality.

I shoved free of his hold and stood.

Then I moved to my pants, yanking them back up and tying the waistband tight.

With a double knot this time.

TEN

Cole

I SHOULD HAVE KNOWN she was going to retreat.

I'd pressed her too hard, too fast, and she'd predictably retreated back into the safety of her shell. That was what any frightened creature would do, not that Olivia was a creature in anything but the most biological way. Still, she was a woman running scared, and we'd just jumped about ten levels on the scale of intimacy.

Maybe she would have been all right if we hadn't had last night or the early hours of this morning. Or the banter as we'd talked. The sharing, albeit minimal of our lives.

Those were ties, and I knew by now that she didn't do that.

Not with the men she was seeing anyway.

With Devon and Becca, it was different.

They were close, but that was an anomaly in Olivia's life and probably mostly because Dev could be a stubborn fuck when he saw someone in his circle that needed care, and he had worn down her barriers.

A pang of jealousy tore through me, but I shoved it down.

Dev didn't know about her horse or the fact that she once hadn't had enough money for food. I would bet my ranch on that. Which meant that she had shared something with me, even though it made her vulnerable.

I watched her tie up her sweats like she was expecting some punk-ass middle-schooler to come behind her and try to pants her. But only when she moved toward Bucky, did I get my shit together. I was still hard, even after the best orgasm of my life, because I'd been dreaming about Olivia for years, and the reality dwarfed the fantasies beyond belief, but I shoved myself back into my underwear and zipped up.

Focus.

She'd made the first move.

She was comfortable with that.

And while I didn't necessarily want her to be *uncomfortable*, I also didn't want her to take this time to shore up her defenses again and shove me into a box that she *was* comfortable with.

That would mean distance and her running.

I got that, really, I did. What we'd just shared was the most intense sexual experience of my life. I'd never had anything be like that—as though I knew what she wanted almost before she did, that I could feel what it was doing to her and it heightened my own pleasure. As though we, two separate people, had become one being for a few moments.

It felt better than anything else. Ever.

But it was also terrifying.

So, I understood the urge for distance, even though I was definitely all in with everything that was Olivia. Still, it was like I had been reaching into the oven for a pan without a potholder, the scorching heat of the metal burning the skin of my hand before I could pull it to safety.

That knee-jerk reaction to yank back was intense.

But I had to shove it down.

I didn't need to run scared, too, not when I knew the potential of us, not when the small pieces of what I'd already learned about her were enough to make me want to tear open her soul and understand every single thing. Fear of getting hurt had never stopped me from playing through pain, from taking another shift, from forcing my burning lungs to work just a little bit harder in order to chase down the puck.

So, no running.

But I also needed to be smart.

Or at least that's what I was thinking before I saw her stumble and start to go down.

Then reason and proceeding carefully with Olivia went out the window.

Hustling, I closed the distance between us and scooped her up again. She'd been favoring her injured foot again, and it took the barest glimpse for me to see that she'd opened the cut back up.

The bottom of her sock was bright red with blood.

"I'm fi—"

I kissed her. She wasn't fine, but I wasn't going to argue with her about it. Hence the kiss, hence keeping her tight against me as I carried her back to the car and set her on the trunk.

Fucking stupid to have done what we'd done, and not just the public part, because that had been risky, but hot as hell. Rather, I hadn't taken care with her injury, and that made me feel like the biggest jackass on the planet. I pulled away once she was on the trunk, bending to retrieve my pack and depositing it next to her.

Also, fucking stupid of me to not have a phone with me.

One call, and I could have had someone out here.

So yeah, stupid was coming at me in a lot of ways that day.

Cursing quietly, I carefully tugged the sock off, pleasantly surprised that my kiss seemed to have distracted her enough that she actually let me tend to her without complaint. Just being able to touch her calmed me enough for the guilt to fade and for me to focus. I just needed to get her foot wrapped and then her on Bucky's back. If we stayed on the main road, it was a straight shot to my house, and we could both ride to make better time.

Buck couldn't handle that forever, but he could make it most of the way.

There. Plan made.

Calm found.

I glanced up into her eyes, saw that her expression had softened, that the panic had disappeared, and in its place was something gentle, almost vulnerable. Maybe she *had* hit her head yesterday. "Olivia?"

"Shh," she murmured, and I froze, head jerking back. I'd expected fire, and definitely running, but instead she gave me something different . . . and something infinitely better. Her fingers brushed my jaw, tone almost reverent. "Thank you for worrying about me. I haven't had much of th—" A shake of her head. "Anyway, I'm fine."

"I've decided that I hate that word," I gritted out.

Still soft. "I know you're freaked out because of the blood, but look, it's not bad. I'm—"

"Do *not* say you're fine."

"Baby." She cupped my cheek. "It's not a big deal."

"You're bleeding."

Lips to my forehead, my jaw. "Just a little bit." Her fingers wrapped around my nape, threading into my hair. "Hush, now."

I'd expected sharp. I'd anticipated harsh. For her to push me away and push hard. Instead, I got soft. Gentle. She knew I was spiraling, feeling like shit that she was hurt because of me and . . . she gave me *soft*.

My breath slid slowly out of me, taking the barbed edges of my emotions with it.

The last of which disappeared when she unzipped the pack and pulled out the first aid kit. "Patch me up, baby. Then let's get out of here."

So, I did. I washed her foot, re-bandaged it, then wrapped the whole thing in gauze because I wasn't about to put a dirty ass sock back on her. And she didn't complain, didn't try to walk when I brought her over to Bucky and set her on his back. No words as I repacked his saddlebags, nor when I mounted behind her and tugged her against my chest, lifting her foot so it was elevated on top of the saddle.

That was when she gave me words.

But they were of the teasing variety, and they soothed the ragged edges of my emotions further.

"Good thing I'm bendy," she said with a chuckle, leaning back against my chest as I picked up the reins and guided Bucky into motion. "This is where I'd say something about being a former gymnast or whatever, but that would be a lie, so I'll just say that I do get my fill of daily yoga, and so that bendy comes in several varieties of flexible."

I snorted, moving us onto the road and finally relaxing enough to joke back, though it was less joke and more self-deprecating truth. "Are you trying to make me hard?"

"Maybe," she said. "Is it working?"

"From the first moment I saw you," I grumbled.

She laughed. "Don't get me started on *my* panties," she teased. "All those half-naked hockey stars and I could barely tear my eyes off you."

"Will you laugh if I admit to keeping my shirt off in hopes of you noticing me?"

"Yes," she said, giggling lightly. "But it worked because I did notice you."

"Well, could have fooled me," I grumbled. "Got a reputation for being that guy, the one always swinging free and loose, hoping that you'd take a second look at me and decide that I was worth your time."

Her breath caught, shoulders stiffening, and I would have thought it was because the road had gotten a little bumpy if not for the way her tone quieted.

"I couldn't," she said. "Couldn't risk noticing you."

My fingers clenched on the reins as I processed that. "I understood."

"Yeah?"

"Yeah," I told her. "I wanted you, but I also got that it wasn't the right time for either of us. You couldn't be seen as the agent who went there with her clients, even if what was between us was different."

"Part of me thinks that even now, I still run that risk," she murmured.

"I know." A beat. "Because even if you only did it once, then there would still be a stigma."

She sighed.

"I don't want to hurt your career."

It was the truth. I didn't want to screw with her professional life, no matter how much I wanted her personally.

She placed her hand over mine on the reins.

"I learned to stop giving two shits what other people thought about me a long time ago." I hadn't realized I'd been holding my breath, but her words had it sliding free. "I know you don't want to hurt me," she said, making my lungs hitch again. "I know you, Cole. That's probably why I've resisted taking what I wanted for so long."

"A lesson in restraint?" I asked.

"Or one in self-punishment," she murmured. "Either way, it's one that's done now."

"Good."

She nestled back against me. "Yes, *good*." A brief pause. "Now, I want you to tell me why a city boy with no horse experience decided to buy a horse as his first big purchase upon making it big."

I chuckled. "You sure you want to hear the sob story?"

"It's better than focusing on my own."

Now wasn't that the truth?

"Okay," I said, knowing that if I ever wanted her to open up to me, I needed to be equally open to her in return. "Most of my life is pretty normal. Parents together, parents divorced. Deadbeat dad who left, and single mom who struggled. We lived on public assistance for a long time. For practically my whole life, I guess." I pressed my lips together for a moment. "One day, I was invited to a party at the ice rink. I think it was the first time I'd ever skated, and a hockey practice was happening after the public skate. I forgot about the party, about the cake and ice cream and favors—and, believe me, for a kid like me, who didn't get that stuff often, forgetting about cake and ice cream and a present my mom didn't have to scrimp and save for was huge."

"Cole."

I paused.

"I understand."

The girl who'd had to sell her horse so her family could eat, certainly did understand.

"Thank you."

She nodded, eyes on the road, but her spine was still pressed to my chest. "So, you fell in love with the sport?"

"Yeah," I said. "I don't know how my mom made it happen, but she got me equipment, paid for my lessons, and I was off." I shook my head, the wonder of her managing that still not old. "I lived at that rink, breathed and bled hockey. And eventually, I managed to make it a career."

"Your mom is so proud of you," she murmured, having spoken to her a few times over the course of my career. I didn't think they'd ever actually met up in person, though, just wreaked havoc over phone lines.

"She is," I agreed. "Got to see me play, and I got to give her a place on the beach, like she'd always dreamed about." I sighed. "Though I damn near had to twist her arm to accept it."

Olivia chuckled. "She's my kind of woman, that's for sure."

"Don't think I forgot what happened the last time the two of you two worked together."

"The team needed baby pictures for their Kids' Night promotion."

My arms tightened around her. "They didn't need a bare-ass naked one of me in the bathtub."

She laughed, full and throaty and, just like that, I was hard again.

And just like that, she noticed.

"Ignore it," I muttered. "Common problem around you."

Her hips shifted. "Kind of hard to ignore it when I know how good it feels inside of me."

Killing. Me.

"Plus, I happen to like your ass, cute baby version or hot adult male variety," she said. "And you still haven't really explained about the horses and the ranch."

I winced. "Didn't forget about that, did you?"

"You subtly avoiding answering a question by offering up other information you're comfortable with sharing?" She turned slightly, blue eyes drifting up to meet mine, a twinkle in their depths. "I think *I* was the one who taught you that trick."

My lips quirked. "Maybe you did."

I paused, loving this part, loving the annoyed little noise she always made in the back of her throat when I made her wait, all the while wondering if she'd make the same sound if I ever summoned up the patience to make her wait before she came.

Maybe once the edge was off . . . though all of that was based on me being able to get between her thighs again.

With Olivia, I couldn't just assume.

However, in this case, she didn't disappoint me and my preconceived notions. She gave me that huff, the little groan that was equal parts sexy and irritated, and snapped, "Spill it, McTavish."

Fuck, I loved that she was full of fire.

"We had an old box TV when I was a kid, a VCR, one movie, and no cable." I leaned a little closer to her, resting my chin on her head and soaking in her scent as I waited for the sound, round two.

She gave it again, but as always with Olivia, she also kept me on my toes, leaning to the side and tilting her head up to nip at my jaw. "You're trying to piss me off."

I rubbed the stinging spot, though her teeth had been more teasing than hurting.

"I like you pissed off."

She grinned and turned forward again. "Dish, Cole."

"Want to guess what that one movie was?"

"I'm guessing it wasn't *Moana*."

I burst out laughing. "No," I said when I could get it out without busting a gut. "It wasn't *Moana*. Probably a good thing or I might have decided that I needed to have sailing as a hobby rather than horses, and boats are even more expensive than these guys—" I patted Bucky's flank. "It was *The Good, The Bad, and The Ugly*."

"Ah."

"Ah?" I asked. "That's it?"

"Yup."

Such a pain in my ass, and I was loving every second of it.

Because then she laughed and relaxed against my chest, and I was inundated with flowers, salt, and the soft woman in my lap, her softly musical voice drifting up, "Clint Eastwood. I get it."

Of course, she did.

"It was escapism," she said. "Not the most moral movie choice for a child to watch growing up, but I'm guessing you didn't exactly understand all of what was going on."

I laughed. "My mom had banned me from watching it, hid it in the cabinet above our fridge when she realized I'd seen it. But you're right. I didn't really get it until I was older. As a kid, all I saw were gunfights and horses." A shrug. "I loved how free they looked. No cars or busy streets. Just open air and freedom and space to roam."

Her breath caught. "Ah," she murmured. "And now I understand the ranch."

"Gives the kids a place to find that," I agreed. She knew we were targeting inner-city kids, those who didn't have the opportunity to go out in nature, maybe had never seen a horse or a campfire. Most had never gone swimming in the ocean or hiked a trail, never had the opportunity to use those as escapes from reality.

Life was shit sometimes.

People and kids needed a way to escape.

And I wanted to help them find it.

I wasn't some noble asshole with a hero complex. I'd just lived that life, had been given some lucky breaks, had experienced generosity, and I wanted to pay it forward in a way I was passionate about.

"You're a good man, Cole," she murmured.

And there it was again, the slight edge creeping into her tone, the verbal expression of her inner turmoil. She was comparing them again and finding herself lacking.

Bullshit.

But *she* needed to see that, to understand that the way she viewed herself wasn't exactly accurate. At least to me.

Now, how to explain that to her without sounding like a high-handed man-splainer.

Impossible.

Sighing, I held her close, vowing to be patient. "Don't think I haven't seen what you've been doing either," I murmured. "You may not be focused on escapism, but you've done a lot for the community."

"Getting some designers to donate old clothes isn't equivalent to building a youth ranch."

"It's a damned good thing, and helping people in your own way," I said. "Plus, I feel like half the time when I tell people I'm working on getting the youth ranch up and running, they think I'm some sort of creeper who's into kids."

She gasped. "People don't think that."

"I've gotten some looks."

"Probably more because they can't understand anyone finding peace out here."

Bucky started to move up hill, nearing the turn off for my house. "And are *you* finding peace out here?" With me? I didn't ask the second aloud, even though I hoped it was true, that I was affecting her as much as she was affecting me.

She was quiet for a long time. "Yes," she eventually murmured. "Surprisingly, I am."

And since she seemed to be answering his unspoken question, that was enough.

ELEVEN

Olivia

WE CRESTED the top of the hill on horseback like the stars of some western movie—I smiled internally as I thought about little Cole watching *The Good, The Bad, and The Ugly* on repeat.

But then that inner smile disappeared, and my breath went alongside it.

The valley was spread out below us, green and lush due to the river snaking through it. Quaint cabins were tucked along one edge, larger buildings on the opposite end. It was a hidden nirvana in a sea of rolling brown hills. I spotted a huge circle of rocks surrounded by benches for campfires, along with a shed near the river that I imagined contained life jackets and swimming gear and fishing equipment. But the most startling visual wasn't the buildings, but nature itself. The way it wove through the camp, the cabins almost blending into the trees.

It was an oasis.

Clink.

One of the chains locked tight around my heart fell to the ground.

Yes, I knew it was a mental manifestation. Yes, it probably meant I was going insane. But no, I also couldn't begin to pretend that what I saw in front of me didn't just mean that Cole McTavish had stolen a piece of my heart.

Fuck.

"It's beautiful," I said, swallowing against the panic.

I'd kept my distance before because I'd had a good excuse. I didn't shit where I ate, and I was a fucking professional. Now, keeping that distance was harder.

Because I'd leaped.

Because the only thing that was keeping my heart safe was the knowledge that he was good, and I was bad, and I couldn't have him permanently.

But *was* I bad?

Was I really?

I'd gone through my whole life with a chip on my shoulder, having spent my childhood being told I was no good, that I wasn't worth much, that I was rotten inside. I'd found my worth in work, but it was also all tied up in that. The job, getting my clients the best deals at any expense.

I worked hard because it had been the only thing I was good at.

And now I wondered if that was gone, who would I be?

I'd always told myself that I was going to work hard and fast and intense until I was fifty, and then I'd retire on a beach somewhere, having done my time. But that imagery never contained another person—or at least not one aside from a cabana boy. Now I wondered if it would be enough. If without the work, I could find my worth in other things.

Was I even capable of that?

Without my career, what was I?

A card house, beautiful and intricate on the outside, but empty and crumbling on the inside?

That was what worried me.

I'd thought I was strong, but then plunk me back into circumstances similar to my childhood and I was losing my mind, breaking down at a nickname, crying over a long-gone horse, fucking a man who'd I'd purposefully kept at a distance because he deserved to find his happy . . . and not with a woman who at thirty-two still didn't really understand the person she was inside.

But had I really tried to understand her?

Or had I grasped onto the first thing that someone had praised me for and then made it my entire life, shunning any distractions that might shatter the illusion?

I . . .

The second.

Fuck, it was the second.

"I—"

I rotated in the saddle to tell Cole . . . something, *anything*. Perhaps to confess, to repent, maybe to scream or cry, but then I saw his face and the pure joy of his expression.

And I knew I couldn't ruin that.

So, I swallowed it down and pointed to the cabins. "Who designed those?"

His eyes warmed as he leaned closer, telling me about the designer, showing me the hidden buildings and parking areas that I'd missed on the first exploration. He told me about the female contractor who was the shit and how she'd managed to source local materials, including the river rocks making up the cabins' facades that were found on a farm that had been sold to developers and was being turned into housing. And he explained what the kids would do when they were there, how the camp manager had loads of ideas for activities and excursions.

It was fucking fantastic.

More chains fell as more realizations struck home. Distance was more than just physical, and while I hadn't slept with Cole, hadn't closed that type of distance until just a few hours before, I realized he'd slowly been weaseling his way into my heart for years.

It wasn't a matter of letting him in.

He already *was* in.

I wanted to be the kind of girl who'd spin in his hold and confess everything I'd just realized. To tell him I'd been in love with him for years and like an idiot, I'd just recognized it, along with the fact that my entire adult life was a sham because I was empty and twisted and dark inside without my job and didn't realize that was all bleeding over into how I viewed myself.

I wanted to tell him I pretended I was confident, but it was a shield.

I wanted to confess I was lonely, but not with him.

I wanted to admit that my mother's words and abuse had broken something inside me, that even though I knew it was unhealthy to still believe the words, that I wasn't sure I would ever be able to logic my way through them, but that I wanted to.

With him.

But I wasn't the kind of girl to confess all.

So I studied the cabins, asked the right questions.

And if I leaned back a little bit more against his chest because it felt incredible to do so, then it was simply incidental contact.

MY FOOT WAS PROPPED on a pillow, the rest of my body secured on Cole's couch with an influx of still more pillows, a glass of wine within reach of my left hand, and a blanket draped over me.

Throw pillows and a blanket.

A woman's touch.

Funny how I didn't like the idea of Cole having been around a woman enough for her to impart her touch on his space.

Okay, not funny. Not at all.

And I was slowly going insane, though I *was* glad to finally be off Bucky's back and reclining on something soft. My foot hurt more than I cared to admit, given the hissy fit I'd thrown over Cole's fussing, not to mention my thighs weren't used to riding . . . a man or a horse.

I'd done plenty of both that day.

Cole's place had been another hour up the trail, something that might have taken twenty or thirty minutes by car, but because there had been two of us on one horse, who wasn't used to carrying two humans, the distance hadn't exactly gone fast.

Or maybe that was because I was mentally spinning.

Me in love with Cole.

That love not making one bit of difference—

Enough.

It was just enough.

I tucked the swirling thoughts deep down in my brain and focused on the beauty of his house. The front was similar to the cabins in the valley, all stone and dark wood, the trees creeping in close enough to camouflage it from view. Inside was all open space and wide windows, cozy furniture, and rustic woodwork. His kitchen practically gave me an orgasm with all the marble and cabinets and the huge ass stove, and I could barely boil water.

But his fireplace was the part that made my heart sing.

Floor-to-ceiling, covered in variations of gray stones, a huge piece of reclaimed wood just above the gas insert set into its middle. No TV above it, just a cozy couch positioned where the warmth of the flames could reach someone lounging on it and a low bookcase perched to one side. I'd already mentioned the loads of pillows and blanket, or rather *blankets*. Definitely a woman's touch there, but also, it was the epitome of lovely, of warmth and comfort . . . and Cole.

"Men," I muttered, wondering when in the hell I'd become this soft.

Probably around the time I'd almost drowned in the ocean and Cole had swept in all strong and hero-like and rescued me.

"What did the male populace do now?"

I jumped, not having heard him cross the room, and tore my eyes from the flames flickering in the fireplace, glancing at him while lifting my glass to my mouth at the same time. To delay, to give me time to think of something quippy and funny to say in return.

Because I couldn't do serious.

"Don't."

I blinked, almost choked on the wine.

"Don't feel like you have to hide from me," he said. "You've always given it to me straight. Let's keep it that way."

"Cole—"

He shook his head. "I'm not saying you need to confess your innermost thoughts, honey, just that you don't need to cover them up with some pithy one-liner." He took the glass and set it on the table. "If you're uncomfortable, I won't press. I just want you to know that I meant what I said before—you get ready to shed that armor, and I'm here to carry it."

My breath caught.

It was a wonder I had any armor left.

With Cole I felt exposed and vulnerable and—

He got that.

After picking the glass of wine back up, he put it back into my hand. "They're doing a dry run at the camp this weekend, so the medic is on his way up. He'll look at your foot. Your car has been towed to the shop in town, but realistically, no one will be in to look at it until Monday. I can drive you back to the city, though, if you need to get back. In the meantime"—he plunked a cell phone into my hand—"a connection with the outside world."

I glanced at the phone then up at him. "Don't you have plans tonight? You don't really want to drive two hours each way, just to get me home. I can call for a car—"

"I would love nothing more than two more hours of your company."

He dropped that declaration there, like it was no big deal, and it took me a minute to catch my breath. It had taken us most of the day to get to his house, and the sun was already starting its downward trek. If the doctor was coming to look at my foot, it would be even later before we left. "By the time you get back—"

"It's not like I had hot plans today, honey," he murmured. "I was camping. Further that, I'm used to late nights, having had my fair share of them."

"But—"

"And if it does get too late, I'll stay at my place in the city."

He had a place in the city?

Cole's thumb brushed over my lips, the latter having parted in surprise. "Yes, I love nature," he said. "No, I don't want to live in it all the time."

Oh.

Oh.

The man was full of surprises.

He grinned. "I do occasionally trade the boots for wingtips and the jeans for suits."

I wrinkled my nose, thinking of the last time I'd seen him in a suit. He'd worn a Christmas-patterned monstrosity to Prestige's holiday party the previous year. "I think I prefer you in jeans."

A brush of his mouth to my jaw. "I don't think jeans would go with those sexy little work outfits you like to wear out." My breath caught, but before I could fumble around to reply with anything, the doorbell rang and Cole straightened, moving away to answer it.

Not disappointment.

I wasn't disappointed that his mouth hadn't found mine.

Hell, who was I kidding? That was *only* disappointment coursing through me, well, disappointment along with an aching need, reminding me that while I'd had Cole once, it was not nearly enough.

Especially as I watched him walk, loose-limbed and confident, graceful for such a big man. It reminded me of how it felt to be in his arms, cradled against his chest.

I wanted more of that.

But could I get my shit together enough to grab hold of it?

I logged into my email while Cole talked with whom I assumed was the doctor at the door a minute, and when the man disappeared back outside with a, "Let me grab my other kit," I quickly typed off a text to Dev, letting him know I was all good, but my car had broken down, along with my cell taking a plunge in the ocean, and that I was borrowing Cole's for the time being.

A reply came back in barely a minute.

I'm glad to hear from you. Couldn't decide if I should be worried you didn't make it or jumping for joy that you'd finally gone off the radar with Cole.

I frowned.

What does that mean?

A few seconds passed before,

You two have been circling each other for years. I'm hoping you at least finally jumped his bones.

My jaw dropped open.

What the fuck, Dev?

His message appeared in my inbox.

You have one life. Cole is a good guy and into you. Live. It.

Then,

I'll get a hold of IT and have a new phone on your desk Monday morning.

I was staring dumbly at the cell when the doctor came back in and crossed over to me. "Olivia?" he asked. "I'm Pete. Heard you hurt your foot."

"I'm fi—"

Cole growled, and I bit back the word almost subconsciously, my mind more focused on what Devon had said. He knew I was into Cole. He'd known? For how long? *Fuck.*

"It's cut," I said. "Though I'm not sure on what exactly," I said, shaking my head to clear it. "I think maybe I just stepped wrong on a rock. It's small, but I reopened it this afternoon when I—"

My cheeks flushed red, and I bit back the words.

Pete glanced at up me, one brow lifting, but he didn't comment, just reached for my foot and began unwinding the seventeen miles of gauze Cole had wrapped around it.

"I cleaned it out the best we could, but I didn't like how deep—"

I stopped listening and hissed out a breath when Pete pressed on both sides of the cut. Fuck that hurt. "Looks like you cleaned it well, but you're right, it is pretty deep. Could use some stitches or glue. Olivia, do you have a preference?"

"Minimal needles," I said. "Not a fan."

"Glue, it is," Pete replied and began pulling supplies out of his kit. "Cole, can you grab a few towels?" Cole nodded and left, but Pete kept talking, the monologue relaxing me. "You keep sipping that wine and lounging there," he said, eyes sparkling. "I'll irrigate this one more time to make sure it's clean and free of foreign objects. Then"—he slipped a blue plastic and paper sheet under my foot—"we'll glue you up and you'll be on your way."

"Easy as that?" I asked.

"Easy as that," he said. "I might even beat you finishing that wine."

I laughed.

"I'll give you some antibiotics. Start them tonight and make sure to finish the full course." He froze and waited for me to nod. "You up to date on your tetanus shot?" He paused a second, and I nodded again. "Good."

By then, Cole was back with the towels and Pete poured a cold solution over my foot, prodding for a few painful moments before drying everything and then gluing the cut closed. He hadn't been kidding about finishing before my wine glass was empty because a few minutes later, I was glued and bandaged and handed a packet of antibiotics—and a few pain pills in case I needed them the following day. Then Pete packed up, giving me the order to stay off my foot for a few days.

"And no Louboutins," Cole muttered.

Pete snorted but nodded. "No heels either."

I rolled my eyes as I downed the rest of my wine, not arguing because the idea of shoving my sore foot into a cramped heel definitely did *not* appeal. I thanked Pete as he and Cole walked to the door then returned my attention to my inbox.

There was one last message from Dev.

Don't be an idiot like I was. Ignore the instinct to run, and leap into the arms of someone who'll catch you. And trust me, Cole's got good hands.

I watched the man in question shake hands with Pete, thanking him and closing and locking the door before picking up the trash and dirty towels and disappearing down the hall.

Capable. Smart.

Kind.

Cole.

I wanted to take Dev's advice.

I just needed to find the strength.

TWELVE

Cole

I HAD A PROBLEM.

And she was sleeping in the seat next to me.

We'd had a fight before we left, her arguing with me about the length of the drive again and how it would be an inconvenience to me. She'd wanted to call a driver to come and pick her up, before I'd just ignored her and began packing up my car and the house for an extended stay in the city.

If I finally had a chance with Olivia Rogers, no fucking way was I going to be two hours away.

I was in the city for the foreseeable future, and that was that.

But now we were approaching said city, and I needed to make a choice. Wake her up to get her address—which I hadn't gotten before sleep had taken her under because she'd been brooding and silent next to me and I'd been trying to find my enjoyment in her irritating the shit out of me—or take her back to my place.

I knew the right thing to do.

It didn't align with what I *wanted* to do.

I always did the right thing, but in this moment, I wanted to do the wrong thing. I wanted Olivia in my space, wanted more time with her, didn't want her to put the walls back up and to have to bust my way through them again.

Not so soon.

Just a little more time.

I took the exit for my building, stopping and going more often than I liked because it was Saturday night in San Francisco, and everyone had decided they needed to be out and about.

About eighteen red lights and two hundred jay-walking pedestrians later, I turned into my parking garage and parked in my spot.

When I turned off my truck, I expected her to wake up, to demand I take her home. But she didn't move, her breathing slow and steady. I reached behind my seat and grabbed my pack then popped my door and hit the pavement.

Still no movement.

If I hadn't just heard her breathing, I would have worried my driving had killed her.

I slung my bag over my shoulder, made sure her antibiotics and pain pills were still in the side pocket then rounded the hood and carefully opened her door. I unclicked her seat belt, scooped her up into my arms, expecting *this* to be the moment that she woke.

Instead, she snuggled into my chest and murmured, "Cole."

My heart skipped a beat.

She'd said my name.

Yes, it was egotistical and so stereotypically male, but I couldn't deny that hearing her murmur my name in her soft and sleepy voice was a shot to the gut. A good one for sure, but it still took my breath away.

"I'm here, honey."

And she settled.

Another gut punch.

Another loss of breath.

When she was unconscious, she trusted me. It was just all of the rest of the time she didn't. I could work with that. I snorted softly, knowing that I'd work with whatever she gave me.

But still . . . layers. This woman had so many of them I knew I'd never get bored.

I closed the passenger's side door, locked up, then carried her to the keypad, inputting my code and pushing my way into the elevators. A swipe of my key fob allowed me to get to the seventeenth floor, which in this case, was also the top floor.

Yes, I drove an old truck.

Yes, I had property in the hills north of the city.

No, that didn't mean I lived in a hovel.

My priorities were location and view, and both the ranch and my condo had them. Ocean on the ranch if I rode Bucky far enough, or if I craned my neck at just the right angle at the condo. Isolation in the hills. Central to everything when I was in the city.

The elevator dinged, and I carried Olivia down the hall.

There were three condos on this floor, and mine was the one in the corner. Lots of glass, lots of unobstructed views of the city, that little sliver of ocean, and maybe on a rare day, if it was clear enough and I found just right the angle to peer through the surrounding buildings, I could catch a glimpse of one arch of the Golden Gate.

But aside from the view, it was merely functional. Couch, television, bed, some basics in the pantry, some clothes in the closet. It wasn't home so much as a place to stay.

I had the feeling it would be more than just a place to stay from now on.

Turning the key in the lock with Olivia in my arms wasn't the easiest thing to do, but I managed without dropping either. Then we were inside, the door was closed behind us, and everything in me settled.

More time. I had it for the moment.

I yanked the covers back and set her on my bed, deciding that I liked her there.

Smiling, I dropped my bag to the floor, unbuttoned my jeans and stepped out of them along with my shoes, then climbed into bed with her. A flick of my wrist brought the blankets up and over us, and then I reached for her, tugging her flush against my chest.

Yeah, I liked her there.

In fact, I decided I was going to keep her there.

Done. Easiest decision of my life.

I woke when it was still dark outside to empty arms and a cold bed.

That I didn't like.

Sitting up, I glanced around my condo, glad it was mostly open space and we hadn't closed the curtains. The city lights shone in, and I spotted her almost immediately. She had a blanket wrapped around her as she stared out the window, one knee cocked, both feet on the floor.

That was the part I really didn't like.

One of those feet should be elevated, not to mention that her ass should be in my bed. I threw back the blankets and got up, closing the space between us and scooping her into my arms.

"Cole—"

I didn't say anything, just carried her back to bed.

"*Cole!*" she exclaimed when I plunked us into it and yanked the covers up again.

"What part of resting that foot don't you understand?" I growled.

She squirmed against my hold. "I wasn't putting any weight on it."

"And how'd you get to the window?" I asked—okay, *snapped*. "You have levitating skills I'm unaware of?"

She shoved hard against my chest. "I've seen you in all varieties of unflattering, Cole McTavish. So, don't you take an attitude with me. I don't like assholes, and I sure as shit don't fuck them."

I was irritated beyond belief, pissed that she'd risk reinjuring her foot after Pete had patched her up just that afternoon.

And I was turned on.

Hard as a fucking rock, because if I loved anything in the world, it was fighting with Olivia.

I knew the exact moment she felt my erection because she froze, bright red fingernail poking into my chest, breath hitching, and eyes going navy. Her hips canted forward, brushing against my cock and making my own breathing short-circuit.

"This is a bad idea," she murmured.

My lips ghosted over hers. "I think we've already discovered it's probably the *best* idea."

"Things between us might get messy."

"*Life* is messy."

Eyes widening, mouth parting. "That's what Dev said."

I huffed out a laugh. "Then I owe him a beer."

"Cocky bastard," she muttered, her sass making a reappearance. "I'm not a sure thing."

"Honey, you've got one thigh thrown over my hips and are grinding your pussy against my dick. If that's not a sure thing, then I don't know what is."

Her growl of outrage was loud, but she didn't lift her leg or back up.

So, I kept talking.

"And if we're talking about sure things, I think we both know where I fall," I murmured, nipping at her earlobe. "I want you, honey, and I'm not going to pretend differently."

Another movement of her hips that was destined to drive me slowly insane. "You're still cocky."

"And *you're* still beautiful."

Lips curving. "Charming man." Her teeth found the sensitive spot just beneath my jaw and bit down hard enough to sting. "Annoying man." Her tongue soothed the spot. "*Dangerous* man."

"Says the woman with her teeth in my skin."

She laughed, full and outright then lay back onto the mattress, tossing her arms above her head. "Okay, Cole. You win. Do your worst."

The cascade of heat down my spine was intense, scorching me from the inside out, cock hardening further, pulse picking up, my breathing doing the same. I went stock-still, but only for a heartbeat because then I got my shit together and moved.

Sweats—hers—off. Shirt—ours—following suit.

Mouth slamming down, hands tracing over the fucking exquisite piece of artwork I'd just unveiled. Beautiful, alabaster skin, rosy nipples pebbled against the sudden rush of air, a narrow strip of hair hiding glistening folds. I almost didn't know where to start.

Olivia smirked up at me, not trying to cover herself. Instead, her arms stretched higher, putting her breasts on display as she grasped onto my headboard.

"Hint," she said. "This is where I want my men to stop eye-fucking me and start *actually* fucking me."

I snorted, ignoring that she'd used the word *men*, and

stroked a finger between her breasts. "We men are visual crea-tures, honey." She shivered as my finger drifted over her belly button, thighs parting when it slid through the strip of hair. "But if you want me to touch"—I dipped it lower, coaxing just the tip through her wetness—"I think I'll start . . ."

She spread her thighs wider now, pelvis tilting, trying to get my finger lower.

I let it move down, flicked it over her clit the same moment that I sucked one of those rosy nubs into my mouth. Olivia screamed, hands coming off the headboard to latch onto my hair, hips thrusting up, hot and damp surrounding my finger.

"*Cole*," she groaned.

I pulled harder, moving my tongue over the tip, loving the way it made her squirm, and cry out, more wet appearing between her thighs.

"That's right, honey," I murmured, kissing my way to the other side. I shifted my hand, letting my thumb circle her clit and the rest of my fingers slip lower, circling her opening, sliding inside. I tried things until I'd discovered what she liked best—two fingers, pressing in and curling forward, slow and steady—then I stayed on target, not deviating, putting all of my focus to good use.

And after years and years of playing a professional sport, I had focus.

I could pick the top corner of the goal from the opposite end of the ice with an arena full of screaming fans, could shoot a slap shot through traffic to hit an open spot of the net. I could also definitely keep finger fucking my woman's pussy while sucking on her glorious breasts, as she squirmed and moved and groaned her way to an orgasm.

And I could do that with my eyes shut.

Not that I was going to do that and miss one glorious second of the show.

A sheen of sweat broke out between her breasts, her skin glistening in the lights of the city. Her head was thrown back on the pillows, shining black silk spread out on the white cotton. I sucked harder, curled my fingers faster, and watched with intense satisfaction as she crested the precipice and flew over the other side.

Her moaning my name as she burst into flames was the sexiest thing I'd ever heard.

At least for about thirty seconds.

Because then she opened hazy eyes and smiled up at me.

"Hi," she said.

My mouth quirked. "Hi, honey."

"I take it back."

I ran my hands up and down her torso, fingers brushing the undersides of her breasts, watching her nipples harden further and goose bumps break out on her skin. "Take what back?"

"You can eye-fuck me all day so long as you attack me like that afterward."

I snorted then lost my battle and burst out laughing. "Fuck, honey."

That laughter lasted all of another thirty seconds.

Because then she reached down and slipped her hand under the waistband of my underwear. Cool fingers encircling me, squeezing hard, pleasure bursting out from my center to shoot down my spine. I groaned, my own hips doing some thrusting of their own. Later, I'd swear I blacked out for a minute because one moment it was just her hand on me, and the next, I was on my back and it was her sexy fucking mouth.

She sucked me deep, taking me in until I bumped the back of her throat.

And she took notes, too, found what I liked and then did it over and over again, driving me higher and higher and generally making me go insane.

But then she twisted her hand, and I almost shot through the roof.

Holy fucking shit.

Insane was nothing compared to her palm and tongue and, *fuck me*, her teeth.

She knew it, too, giving me a run for my money when it came to focus, taking me so close to the edge that I nearly toppled over. But fuck if I was going to come without being inside her. I grabbed her under her shoulders and yanked, bringing her up so her mouth was crushed against mine. Tongue shoving home, I flipped us, tucked her legs up and thrust home.

"Cole! Fuck!"

I froze, red hazing the edges of my vision, worried I'd hurt her. "Honey?"

"Give a girl a warning, why don't you?"

Teasing, though her cheeks were flushed scarlet. I relaxed. "No," I said and bent my head to suck one nipple into her mouth, "I don't think I will."

She cried out, pussy clenching around me, wet gushing to coat my cock, and I lost the tendrils of control I'd been holding on to. They burned away like tissue paper, insubstantial and gone in an instant.

I began moving, glad she was right there with me, hips matching mine, nails digging into my shoulders, groans echoing in my ear.

It wasn't slow and steady. It wasn't gentle.

It was raw and intense and fucking incredible.

Then it was incendiary.

Deep, hard, *wet*, sweat dripping down my brow, nails scouring down my spine hard enough to hurt. But even that was incredible, sending my pleasure skyrocketing and any rational thought out of my mind as I pounded into her.

Olivia stiffened, keening moan filling the air, fingers digging in, legs locking tight.

"Oh fuck," she groaned. "Oh fuck. Oh fuck. *Oh fuck, Cole!*"

Her pussy clenched tight as she came, and thank God for that, because I was right there with her, desire burning a path down my spine as I exploded inside her.

It took me a long moment to feel my arms and legs again, but eventually I did regain feeling and I rolled us to my side. I was still hard and still inside her, but Olivia didn't seem to mind.

She just curled up against my chest and released a huge breath.

A shaking breath.

A wet, shaking breath.

"Honey," I murmured, worry clouding my voice. I'd hurt her. Fuck. "Did I—?"

She sucked in air, released it slowly. "Not you, Cole," she said softly.

I bit my tongue, wanting to ask. But I'd promised not to press, promised to wait for her to give me only what she was willing.

Her hand flattened out, resting on my chest above my still slowing heart.

"It's just that I find my armor isn't impenetrable when it comes to you."

"*Honey.*"

"Shh, Cole," she said. "That's all I can give tonight."

"It's enough, honey. It's more than enough."

I pressed a kiss to her forehead, slipping briefly out of bed to clean us both up before I gathered her back into my arms and held her tight, watching the city lights until sleep took us both under.

THIRTEEN

Olivia

I WAS WEARING FLATS, and I was not happy about it.

Cole and I had slept late then had brunch together at a tiny restaurant around the corner from his condo. Then we'd gone back to his place and had sex again. It was just as good as the previous two times, only slower because we both had had at least a modicum of self-control.

Which meant I'd let Cole kiss me first.

And not on the lips . . . or well, not on the lips on my mouth anyway.

The memory of that made me smile, the slight ache between my thighs a pleasant reminder. He'd been thorough in his kissing, adept at proving his skills, particularly good with his tongue and keen on proving it.

Insatiable man.

Insatiable *me*.

But I was still in flats.

Because the sneaky butthead had gotten together with Devon to confiscate my heels. He hadn't said a word either, had just let me get into the Lyft I demanded to take late the night before and dropped me with a kiss at the door, all while knowing that Dev had stopped by my place earlier in the day and had packed up every shoe that had the least bit of style.

If I didn't love him, I'd want to punch him.

Hell, I wanted to punch him anyway.

Especially when he'd responded to my angry voicemail I'd left at zero-dark-thirty that morning with a kissy face emoji.

A kissy face.

Sighing, I flopped back in my chair, mentally cursing him, while also understanding the fact that I'd just thought the dirtiest three words in my vocabulary—I, love, and him—without combusting or spiraling meant that I'd taken some big steps in the last few days.

I loved him.

I was wary as fuck about the emotion and what it might mean for our friendship, the risk it posed to my heart, but I'd at least opened my eyes to recognize there was a reason he'd stuck in my life through the years.

Not many people did.

Becca. Devon. Cole.

I loved them all.

I only wanted to fuck Cole. That was only the slightest difference between what I felt for Devon and Becca, right? I mean, they were both gorgeous and totally fuckable for sure. Cole was just—

"Ugh," I muttered, letting my head fall back and my eyes slide closed.

"It can't be that bad," Dev said, "I've seen your shoe collection, and your flats are adorable."

I was standing even before he finished teasing, making my way around my desk in bare feet because—and I would admit this over my cold dead body—the cut hurt when I crammed my foot into any shoe, let alone one suitable for work.

I'd even considered slippers that morning for a hellish moment before I'd come to my senses.

What? I liked my heels, dammit.

"You"—I pointed at him with narrowed eyes—"are in on Cole's scheme and so are dead to me. He"—I smiled at the little nugget in the car seat, staring up at me, serious eyes so much like Devon's that they nearly stole my breath—"on the other hand, is the only male I'm willing to forgive."

"Forgive?" Dev asked, not fighting me when I grabbed the car seat and set it on the floor, intent on retrieving Jasper from baby jail.

"Yes, forgive," I said firmly, kneeling as I cuddled Jasper close. "I had to wear a skirt because all of my pants are too long."

His brows drew together, mouth opening—

"Forget it," Becca said, breezing into my office and shutting the door. "You'll never understand." She brushed her finger down Jasper's cheek. "Hey, sweetie," she murmured, and I felt my uterus clench for the first time in . . . well, ever.

I wanted one.

Holy fucking shit. I *wanted* one.

What? How? Since when did I think like that?

Cole.

"Fucking Cole."

I didn't realize I'd said the last aloud until I glanced up and saw both Becca and Devon's eyes on me. I'm sure panic was written on my face because Dev immediately straightened, gaze concerned, body language tense. But Becca, fucking incredible woman and assistant she was, knew immediately what was bothering me.

She scooped Jasper out of my arms and tucked him into

Dev's. Then she opened the door. "Out. The bottle I pumped for him is on your desk."

Dev started out, stopped on the threshold. "Is everything—"

"Go." She closed the door, flipped the lock. "Tell me absolutely everything."

Heart and mind reeling from the assault of my memories two days before, from the emotional interlude with Cole and me realizing my long-held feelings for him, to Jasper and how I'd just realized that beneath the shield of work and distance I might actually want a family someday.

"My dad died when I was ten, but it all began long before that," I admitted. "I think my mom was jealous of our relationship or maybe competitive. She didn't like it when we spent time alone together at all. And at first, it was the little comments. I was pushy, sassy, overconfident." I shook my head. "My dad talked to her, but things didn't get better. She just didn't say them around him. She'd wait until he was at work to tell me I was selfish and needy."

Becca touched my arm when I faltered. "A child wanting to spend time with her parent isn't needy or selfish."

"I know," I murmured. "Or, I guess *logically*, I know. It's easy to see that as truth as an adult, but I hear her voice in my head when I'm with Cole. Her telling me that I'm rotten to the core, that I was the reason my dad worked so hard, why he died of a heart attack."

"Viv."

I bit my lip. "I know," I said, and my eyes stung. "It wasn't my fault, but . . . I keep thinking that . . ."

"Something might happen, and you'll be the reason why Cole gets hurt."

I sniffed. "Fuck. It's so stupid. He's the one guy who's stuck in my life, the one who I've made sure sticks, and I'm so fucking scared of being with him and screwing things up."

"No," she said gently. "You're afraid of letting him in. Afraid he'll see everything and that you won't be what he wants."

I slumped back against my desk. "Yeah. That. So much for being a strong, powerful, confident woman, huh?"

"Feelings don't make you weak, Viv."

"Sure feels like it," I grumbled.

"They can suck, that's for sure. But you know what makes that suckage better?"

"No."

"Letting someone else in to share the burden."

"Ugh," I muttered, plunking my head against the wood. "Why did I know you would say that?"

"Because I'm brilliant." She scooted next to me, bumped my shoulder with hers. "And you are, too. That's why you're recognizing that the thought processes in your head right now aren't healthy."

"That's the fucking understatement of the year."

Becca dropped her head to my shoulder with a soft laugh. "I love you, babe."

I sucked in a breath, let my head rest on top of hers. "I love you, too."

"And just like that, feelings."

"And just like that, fired."

She snorted. "Yeah right, you'd miss me too much, Viv."

Since she was right about that, I didn't comment, just wrapped my arms around her and hugged her tight. After a long moment, I sighed and disengaged, helping her to her feet once I'd found my own.

"Fine," I said, lips twitching. "You're rehired."

She flicked her hair over her shoulder. "I don't even know if I *want* to be rehired," she said and then laughed at what must have been a crestfallen expression on my face. "I think your little man-child of an assistant might shape up yet. And if not, I have a few feelers out. Though next time, you'll let me do the hiring."

I wrinkled my nose. "I would have let you do that if the baby hadn't come two weeks early."

"I would have hired someone sooner if you weren't in denial. Then I could have trained my replacement fully before I had Jasper."

"Fine." I lifted my palms in surrender. "You win."

A beatific smile. "I know. Now," she said. "I know I'm not technically on the clock, but my assistant switch didn't just flick off because I pushed out a kid, so I've got a two-step plan for Operation Cole."

"He gives fantastic oral sex," I blurted.

Becca grinned. "I'm glad to hear it, but that's not on the two-step plan."

Damn.

"Don't look so disappointed," she said and held up her cell. "First order of business is an appointment with Dr. Larsen."

"Is she a sex therapist or something?"

Becca laughed. "Something on your mind you'd like to share with the class, Viv honey? Besides his superior oral skills?"

I shook my head, cheeks warm, but Becca and I had shared enough at this point that I wasn't critically embarrassed. Especially when it was clear that I did have sex on the brain.

Three times with Cole wasn't enough.

And what did that say about me, that sex was okay, but the other intimacies were frightening as hell?

Okay, that *was* true.

"He has a big dick?" I said.

Becca snorted. "Why is that phrased as a question? He does or doesn't?"

"Oh, he does," I said and groaned, leaning back against my desk. "I'm so messed up, I don't even know what I'm saying."

"He's got you twisted up into all sorts of knots, that's for sure. This"—she held up her phone again—"will help. Dr. Larsen is my therapist."

My breath caught.

"Bec—"

"I struggled when Dev and I couldn't get pregnant, kept internalizing everything, thinking it was my fault, my failures." She took both of my hands in hers. "Then all the stuff from my past kept creeping in and coloring all of my interactions. Dev was great," she said. "You know how he is. Always has my back, totally on my side. Just like Cole will be. But I couldn't just take his words at face value. I knew he loved me, knew that would make him forgive almost anything." She squeezed my fingers lightly. "Eventually, I realized I needed someone outside of the pair of us to talk to. Someone impartial, who wouldn't judge the spiraling thoughts in my head. And I found Dr. L. You'll like her, Viv. Trust me."

"I—"

"I made an appointment for you with her this afternoon. Or rather, you're taking my appointment so you can get in right away." Her eyes narrowed. "And then you're giving me my time slot back and finding your own."

"I—"

"And no arguing, missy. You'll go and talk to her, and you'll like it."

"I—"

"I *said* no arguing."

"*Becca.*"

"What?" she snapped, clearly still expecting me to argue.

Instead, I hugged her. Tightly. "Thank you," I whispered in her ear.

Silence then, she whispered back, "No problem."

"Can you make me one promise, though?" I asked as I dropped my arms.

"Maybe."

I chuckled, knowing that she'd bend over backwards for practically anything I asked, so long as I went to the appointment.

"Can we maybe try to confide in each other, too?" I asked, suddenly nervous that I was requesting something she didn't want to give. Becca and I were close, had been close for a while, but I was also just realizing that close wasn't measured in equal parts. She could know how I preferred my coffee, my favorite color of lipstick, that I preferred my meetings after lunch, so I could take care of emails in the morning. But though I could tell anyone her preference for lunch places, and even how she liked her signature line in emails to look, we hadn't discussed our pasts. Even on a most basic level, she hadn't known about my parents until a few minutes ago, and I hadn't even begun to realize she'd thought the infertility was her fault.

I didn't want that to continue.

I wanted more.

I think that was the biggest change in my thinking over the last few days. That water closing over my head, the panic in not being able to escape, and then finding my rescue in Cole's arms had shifted things around inside of my heart, my mind. I'd thought it was simply fear of almost dying at first, hadn't realized that it was actually *Cole* being there in that moment, when I'd needed him, and then not lording it over me, not making it be anything other than him seeing a person struggle and reaching out a hand to help. But *that* was Cole crystallized down to his inner essence, and that moment had changed things for me. I'd been vulnerable, my armor weakened enough to let him in. I'd lashed out, pushed him away, and he'd taken everything I'd thrown at him easily. He'd *handled* me.

Me.

A woman who would have said it was not something I enjoyed, had taken pleasure in someone looking out for me. I loved how he smiled at me, eyes warm, lips twitching, loved the heat in his expression when I threw sass his way, loved that he seemed to take each of my moods as something to be enjoyed and not something to merely be tolerated.

But the thought of that enjoyment fading, of losing that smile, the warm eyes, still tied my stomach into knots.

And . . . *that* was why I needed to talk with Dr. Larsen.

Becca tugged the end of my ponytail. "Asking me questions when your mind is a million miles away again?"

"I-I'm s—" I stammered, guilt pouring through me. She was right. I—

She tugged again. "*I'm teasing.* I know you, Viv, and that's how I know you were furiously thinking about something else." A beat. "But it's also how I know you were doing it thinking about something important." Her hands dropped onto my shoulders. "We know a lot about each other," she said softly. "But you're right. It's time we learned the really important stuff, too."

Relief slid down my spine, and I smiled at her. "You mean something more important than shoe size?"

She rolled her eyes. "Yes, Viv. I mean more than shoes."

"Becca?" I asked when her hand was on the doorknob.

"Yeah?"

"You said it was a two-part plan."

"Yeah, I did."

I hesitated. "So, what's the other part?"

Gentle eyes met mine over her shoulder. "Viv honey, the other part is that you open up to Cole. That you give him everything and let him help you through to the other side."

My breath caught.

"Steady."

I nodded.

"You got this."

Another nod, but I wasn't as sure as the action depicted. And of course, Becca knew that, too, because she smiled and waved a hand. "Never said the plan didn't take big ole lady balls."

My lips twitched. "That's true."

She waved and opened the door, pausing on the threshold to call back, "By the way, Viv, yours are the biggest I've ever seen. Just make sure you use them."

I opened my mouth to call something back, but my new phone buzzed in my hand, and I glanced down at the screen to see a calendar invite with the appointment time and location of Dr. Larsen's office.

The woman was efficient.

Thank God for that.

I accepted the invite then sat at my desk. I had emails and contract offers to get through, followed by a future life to build.

It was all just in a normal woman's workday.

No big deal.

FOURTEEN

Cole

I STARED down at my phone, rereading the transcription of the message Olivia had left that morning, threatening to dismember me because I'd teamed up with Dev to hold her heels in jail, when it rang.

Olivia in real time. Perfect.

I grinned and quickly swiped to answer it. "Hey, honey."

Her voice was raspy and filled with emotion. "Hey."

My gut sank. "Baby, what's the matter?"

She sniffed. "I-I can't come over tonight."

I straightened, jumping off my couch and pacing the across the front room for the apartment. I had DoorDash on the way, flowers on the table, a new pair of Louboutins wrapped and by the couch.

And Olivia was panicking.

"What's happening?"

Silence in response, and I made a decision.

"I'm coming over."

"What?" she gasped. "You don't even know where I live."

"Then tell me or I'll call Devon and find out," I said, shoving my feet into boots. "I'm not leaving you alone Olivia. I know we still have a lot to work out, but that doesn't mean you get to just push me away."

"I can do what I want, Cole," she snapped, and relief poured through me when the fire returned to her tone. "I'm a grown woman."

"You tell me your address or I'm calling Dev."

"I'm not—"

"Calling Dev then," I growled and hung up, immediately tapping the screen rapidly to contact my friend and agent.

"Yo," Dev said.

"I need Olivia's address."

Dev's tone grew cold. "What did you do?"

I strode to the front door. "Fuck you, Dev. I didn't do anything. We're trying to see where this thing is between us and she's panicking and pushing me away. I'm not going to let her."

Silence. Fuck, I really hated quiet. At least that particular day.

"You sure you didn't do—"

There was fumbling and a squawk and then Becca was on the line. "She went and talked to someone today. A therapist. She might be raw and need to be alone."

My heart skipped a beat. "The last thing she needs to be is alone. Her dad died and her mother took it out on her. She needs people who love her to be there for her. Which means she needs *me*."

"Cole—"

"Don't try to talk me out of it. If this is the first time she's talking to someone about everything in her past then she needs me. Okay? Case closed, so give me the fucking address."

"Cole—"

"No arguments."

"*Cole!*"

"What?" I snapped.

"I'm trying to tell you I'll text you her information."

"Oh." A beat. "Thanks."

"Tread carefully, Cole."

"Always."

I hung up the phone, feeling it buzz just as I locked my front door. Five minutes later I was in my truck and on my way to her place.

Trouble was, she didn't answer the door when I made it there.

FIFTEEN

Olivia

HE WAS KNOCKING at my door.

And I was hiding in my closet.

"Becca," I whispered into my cell phone. "He's here."

"Go answer the door, you idiot," she snapped, and I couldn't exactly fault her for her tone. Before calling Becca and explaining the situation in broken, frantic statements, I'd spent the previous five minutes since he'd begun knocking flailing around like a panicked, irrational woman.

And I despised irrational women.

Maybe more than actually *being* one.

Case in point, I was so off my game, I wasn't even annoyed with myself when I said, "I can't. I'm splotchy from crying and am wearing *the* sweatpants."

My sad, holey, frumpy, only-worn-during-my-period sweatpants. They were easily the most unflattering garment I owned.

Becca sighed. "I've seen the horror of said sweatpants and can only advise that Cole will not give two shits about them. He's worried about you. *Go answer the door.*"

"I—"

"Hang up and *go*."

I hung up and went.

The lock had barely clicked open before Cole was pushing through, eyes blazing and lips pressed firmly together. "What the fuck, Olivia?"

"Go away, Cole. I don't need to deal with your shit."

"Maybe not," he said, "But I'm going to be here for you to deal with anyway."

"*I don't need you!*" I shrieked, part of me not even sure why I was yelling, the rest of me knowing that he might as well see me at my worst because then he'd realize I wasn't good enough for him and he'd leave.

It would hurt like hell, but at least I'd be okay.

"Well, *I* need you."

I froze, blinking up at him. Then the old ice came back, protecting that vulnerable core that felt flayed open from the weekend, from rehashing my childhood with Dr. L. She'd advised me not to make any rash decisions about my life for a few days, that I would probably feel on edge.

But fuck it.

This was me. This barbed bitchy woman was all I'd *ever* be.

Might as well bare it all before Cole, let him be fully aware of what he was inheriting.

I scoffed, turned away. "Sure," I said. "Keep telling yourself that. You just want an easy lay around, one who'll give it up without protest and deep throat you on command."

"*What the fuck, Olivia?*" he said again, but this time it was more growl than worried and annoyed. He was pissed off and part of me was glad for that.

Now he'd leave.

But he didn't.

Instead, he grabbed me, yanked me against his chest, and

banded his arms around me. I expected angry words in my ear, vitriol blasting my ear drums, but he just held me, one hand drifting gently up and down my back.

And that was when the tears came.

I sobbed into his chest. I sobbed as he picked me up and carried me to the couch. I sobbed as he gently kissed the tears away.

I sobbed until there were no more tears.

Then I lay quietly against his chest, wondering how in hell to explain how important this moment was to me. I'd pushed him away again. I'd been trying to don that armor.

And he stayed. He'd kept that armor on its hooks and wouldn't let me wear it.

Scary. Also, wonderful.

"I was a bitch," I eventually rasped. "I'm sorry."

He brushed his thumb under each of my eyes in turn, wiping away the tears. "Weren't you the one who said that was a good thing?"

That startled a little chuckle out of me and then another when my stomach rumbled, and he pulled out his phone, asking, "DoorDash?"

I nodded, eyes glued to my manicure, embarrassed that I'd become so unhinged and feeling extremely guilty I'd screamed at him. "I shouldn't have yelled. I'm so—"

He kissed me.

"No apologies, okay?" he murmured. "This is a lot. Becca mentioned . . . well, she said you'd gone to talk to someone. That's a good thing."

"I don't think it can be good if it made me go so far off the rails."

"It's good because you got it out." He sighed then said softly, "For a long time, I thought my dad leaving was my fault, thought it would have been easier if my mom had just dropped me off in foster care and started over."

I shifted around, touched his cheek. "*Cole.* Your mom—"

"I know," he said. "She cornered me when I was a teenager, made me talk it out with her. It wasn't an easy conversation—no, *conversations,* because she made sure to rehash it with me many times over until I understood she didn't view raising me as a sacrifice." He covered my hand with his, warm and strong and a little rough. But that was Cole. "I thought she was going to tan my hide for even thinking it," he murmured. "But eventually I managed to stop blaming myself and recognize the gift she'd given me."

"Are you saying you're a gift?"

He smirked. "Absolutely."

I chuckled then sobered, touching his cheek again. "I'm not sure I'm ready to talk about it yet."

"I'll be here when you are." A beat as he held up his phone. "Now, should we order Chinese or Italian?"

"Italian," I said without hesitation. "Tears mean I need carbs."

"Roger that." He began moving his finger across the screen, putting in exactly what I would have ordered myself. Somehow, that wasn't a surprise.

Cole knew me.

He also knew when I was giving him shit.

"Tan your hide? Your *The Good, The Bad, and The Ugly* is showing."

He pressed the button to send the order then tossed his phone on the coffee table and pinned me to the couch, wide grin on his face. "Promise you'll never stop giving me shit."

"Now *that's* a promise I can—"

Cole cut me off with a kiss . . . and kept kissing me until the food showed up at my door.

SIXTEEN

Cole

"I'LL ONLY GIVE these to you if you promise to forgive me for holding your shoes hostage."

It was a week from the day I'd stormed into Olivia's apartment and we'd finally made it back to my place. I'd stayed until she'd fallen asleep that fateful night, wondering exactly what she'd talked to the therapist about and why it had destroyed her defenses so thoroughly.

But I'd promised her patience.

And so I waited.

Meanwhile, I'd managed to sneak into her office with lunch twice and back over to her place one other time. The other two nights I'd been putting fires out at the ranch and meeting with management at the Gold about developing their youth program.

Looked I'd be spending more time in the City.

I grinned. Olivia would have to get used to having me around.

Now, it was the following Monday and I held up the box of

Louboutin's I'd had previously wrapped up for her like they were the greatest treat in the universe.

I should face it, to Olivia they basically were.

"Present!" she chirped, clapping her hands together. "Give it here!"

I held the box aloft. "Not until you say the words and forgive me for all transgressions committed against your shoes."

She glanced up at him, eyes twinkling. "I'm not sure I can. I'm not exactly known as a forgiving woman." Olivia took a step closer, breasts brushing his chest. "I'm—" She kissed my jaw, made a sneaky grab for the present.

I snatched it back, holding out it of reach. "I'm taller," I said as she jumped and tried to snag it out of my hand. "It's not gonna work."

She stuck out her bottom lip, pouting, but one of her palms was sliding down his stomach, fingers tugging at the button on his jeans. "I know *something* that'll work."

My lips twitched. "Trouble." But I brushed her hand away and handed her the box anyway.

The noise she made when I opened the box had my cock twitching.

She tore open the paper and touched the label on the lid almost reverently. *"You didn't."*

I shrugged. "Becca told me which ones you didn't have. I hope she was right."

Not that Dev's wife was often wrong, especially when it came to important things like her former boss's shoes.

"She was right. I don't have these ones," Olivia said, slipping off her own black pumps and swapping them for the black and red polka dot pair Becca had advised me to get. Personally, I'd wanted to get her the fire engine ones that matched the lipstick she always wore, but had been assured she already owned that exact pair.

Now to bribe her into wearing them both for me . . . and nothing else.

Good plan.

"You like them?" I asked.

In answer, she launched herself into my arms, slamming her mouth down onto mine. "I love y—*them*," she said, when she'd pulled away. Her cheeks went pink at the words, eyes darting to her hands.

But I didn't call her on the slip. It was enough that she might possibly be thinking the words, and having the feelings in the first place.

"Try 'em on?" I asked, waggling my brows.

Her eyes found mine again, and she lightly smacked my chest. "You just want to play fashion show."

"That's a thing?"

Her smile turned wicked as she reached for the top button of her blouse. "It's definitely a thing and *this* present might have earned you a *semi-naked* fashion show."

"Only semi?" I stuck out my bottom lip.

"Don't press your luck." Rising on tiptoe, she nipped at my jaw. "Hell, who am I kidding? It'll most certainly be *mostly* naked."

I laughed. "I'll try and tempt you into *totally* naked."

A few buttons came undone. "I think that can be accomplished."

Turned out she was right.

And the next night, I was able to accomplish something else —fashion show number two meant seeing those sexy red heels on her feet . . . and nothing else.

Yeah, my woman was the shit.

SEVENTEEN

Olivia

I WAS COOKING dinner for the man I was dating.

That in of itself was a novelty.

Or maybe a comedy, since I regularly burned water. No seriously, I burned *water* on a regular basis.

The kitchen in my apartment was lovely, with marble countertops and built-in appliances, but it was also virtually unused because I'd had to hire a special cleaning company to come in and work their magic after the last time I'd partaken in cooking activities.

That had been to boil some water because I'd been craving old school Kraft macaroni and cheese.

It had also been the reason I'd met Steph and her kiddo, Sam, so I couldn't be *too* disappointed in myself. Her and her crew had come in to deep clean my place and they'd done such a good job, I'd conned her into working for Prestige.

Burning water sometimes brought good things.

Life has a way of working out, Dr. L had said that day during our appointment and she was right. I'd been telling her how I'd scored the internship, after having randomly met the former owner of Prestige Media Group while working my way through junior college as a barista. He'd appreciated my attention to detail, how I'd remembered the regular clients' names and orders.

And he'd offered me a job.

Since it had paid about three times my salary at the coffee shop and didn't require me to wake up at four in the morning, it had been a no brainer.

Turned out I was good at getting coffee for the staff and players at Prestige, and even better at remembering obscure details about contracts.

Because of a coffee . . . or rather, because of many good coffees over the course of several months, my life had changed. But still, I'd stumbled onto an opportunity, hadn't balked, and instead seized it. Then I'd proved myself and worked hard.

Dr. L said that I could do the same with Cole.

Hence the cooking and trying to win his heart via his stomach.

Wasn't that what girlfriends did?

I bit my lip, hoping that I could be girlfriend material and also hoping that mac and cheese went a little better the second round. This time I was guarding the boiling pot, not daring to leave it and risk getting distracted by emails again, definitely not wanting to have to buy a new saucepan because I'd reduced it to a melted puddle on the stovetop.

I'd also had to buy a new stove.

Cute.

Snorting, I opened the blue box and poured in the contents just as the water began boiling. Good job me.

Of course, dumping the entire contents also meant that I dunked the packet of fake cheese in the boiling water as well.

"Oh boy, Rogers," I muttered, fishing it out. "Get it together." I flipped over the box to reread the cooking instructions. A girl couldn't be too careful when it came to making mac and—

My heart sank as I realized what was printed there.

I needed butter *and* milk? I'd thought it was one or the other.

"Shit," I muttered, opening my fridge, and pretending that milk might have mysteriously appeared in the twenty minutes since I'd been home. It hadn't, and the couple of minutes I spent searching for it proved to be my downfall.

I sniffed.

"*Shit.*"

I slammed the fridge door closed and sprinted to the stove. The pot was boiling over. I turned down the heat, but the damage had been done.

I had a burnt brick of pasta in the pan.

Knock. Knock. Knock.

"Oh for fuck's sake." I shoved the pot off the heat and answered the door. Cole was there, a bouquet of flowers in his hand. But it wasn't the collection of sunflowers there that made my heart skip.

Nope. It was the bag from Molly's in the other one.

He gave me a sheepish smile. "Just in case."

"*Cole.*" I rose on tiptoe and kissed him.

His lips parted, tongue sweeping into my mouth and making heat spiral from the inside out, and he nudged me back into apartment, closing the door behind us. Then he dropped the flowers and food on the table I had there, pulled me close, and reminded me how much I loved his mouth.

Loved *him.*

Eventually, we had to break apart for oxygen—damn fallible human bodies—and I stepped back out of his arms. "I need to finish cooking dinner."

One brow lifted. "Is that what I'm smelling?" he asked cautiously.

"It's delicious," I said, pretending to not notice the rather unpleasant scent from the kitchen mixing with the yumminess from the bag of goodies he'd brought. "I hope you brought your hungry pants—"

He snagged me by the waist, tugged my back to his chest, and nipped my ear. "I brought you brownies." Another nip. "And soup."

I shivered. "I made—"

His hand cupped my breast. "Did I mention *brownies?*"

"I really think we should eat what I made—"

"I'll eat *you* later if you throw that repulsive-smelling meal in the trash where it belongs."

"*Cole!*"

"Come on, honey," he coaxed, nibbling along my jaw.

And because I was fucking with him—the bag from Molly's would have convinced me to throw away *anything* I was cooking, even if it hadn't already been a disaster—I nodded. "Okay, you've finally convinced me."

"Liar," he said, laughing. "But now I win both ways."

I spun in his arms, staring up at the only man who'd ever managed to get the best of me, the only one who'd ever been able to weasel his way into my heart, and my lips parted.

This was when I should express what I was feeling.

This was my chance to grasp on and—

My stomach knotted.

I couldn't do it.

Not yet. Not—

Cole put me out of my misery by kissing my forehead. "I'll get the pot, you get the food. Meet you at the table."

"I—"

He nudged me forward. "Do you want wine?"

I forced out a laugh, touched by his understanding and really fucking disappointed in myself that I couldn't push beyond this fear. "I'll never turn down wine. The opener is in the—"

"I've got it. As long as you promise to save me at least *one* brownie."

"That's a promise I can't keep, McTavish."

He laughed. "I'll hurry then."

"Good luck," I called teasingly, grabbing the bag and jogging to the table. The plastic crinkled as I rifled through the contents.

Cole made it to the table in record time, two glasses of red wine in his hands, warmth in his expression.

Because I'd saved him *two* brownies.

Progress, see?

"I'M SO FREAKING PATHETIC," I said. "I can think I love him, can feel it in my heart. Hell, I can tell *you* the damn words and yet I can't tell him."

Not that *he'd* said them either.

But then again, he didn't have the same hang ups I did.

Dr. L sighed and leaned back in her chair. "I think you're being too hard on yourself. You've made a lot of progress over this last month and a half."

Not enough to tell the man who'd become incredibly integral to my life that I had big feelings for him. *Huge* feelings. Giant, ginormous—

Well, that was a lot of synonyms, but the point was, my head was ready to leap and yet my heart was still holding back.

And he knew it.

He was being patient and not pushing, but every time I opened my mouth to tell him how much he meant to me—not even necessarily the big three words—I faltered, either clamming up or making some stupid joke and changing the subject.

.   I just couldn't go through with it.

"Why do you think it's so hard for you to tell him what he means to you, but easy for you to show him?"

I snorted. "That's easy. Actions speak louder than words."

"Stop," Dr. L said. "And think. *Of course*, actions speak louder than words. While it's good you're showing him how important he is to you . . . humans also need words. You have to consider that at some point you two won't be able to move forward without them."

Damn.

"You're right."

She laughed. "You don't have to sound so happy about it."

I sighed and leaned back in the chair, groaning. "I just don't want to be broken anymore."

She reached across the table, patted my hand. "That's the thing. You're *not*. You never were. People aren't broken. They get hurt, yes, damaged, even. But you're none of those things, Olivia." Her voice gentled. "What you are is scared."

I sighed. "That's not exactly something I don't know."

"So why can you burst through every other barrier in your life, but not this one?"

"Ugh," I exclaimed, seeing where she was going with this and feeling like it was just spinning me in circles I'd already been around. "He's important. He can hurt me. He—"

I froze and she nodded encouragingly.

"He . . . reminds me of my dad."

Dr. L sat back. "Bingo."

My eyes burned, heart clenching and stomach knotting. "I'm scared to take the final step because if things don't work out, it'll be like losing my dad all over again."

"And," she murmured. "If things *do* work out and something

happens to him, it'll be the same." She paused and I felt tears spill down my cheeks. "But what you have to consider is if having half of happy with Cole is enough."

I shook my head, sob catching in my chest. "It's not," I said through my tears. "I want *all* of him."

"And *there's* your motivation to push through."

I sniffed, dashing my hands across my cheeks. "But what if I can't do it?"

"Then eventually you'll lose him," she said, matter-of-factly. "Is that something you can handle?"

My eyes were malfunctioning, that was why the fucking tears wouldn't stop. Either that, or I'd just had the breakthrough I was looking for. "N-no." I sniffed. "But I also don't think I could handle loving him even more and *then* losing him in the end."

"That, unfortunately, is the risk we all take with relationships."

"Fuck." My chest constricted.

"They're not for the weak." She squeezed my hand again. "But you're not weak, are you, Olivia?"

I hung my head for a long moment, pushing down the sobs, wiping away the tears. "No," I murmured. "I'm not."

"I'm a bad ass bitch."

Dr. L nodded. "Exactly."

EIGHTEEN

Cole

"MOM?" I said, swiping my finger across the screen and answering her call. She didn't tend to phone during the week—leaving our weekly chats to Sundays—unless something was up. "Is everything okay?"

Her voice was warm sunshine and my childhood all at once, especially when the tone went slightly scolding. "You're asking *me* that?" she accused. "*You're* the one who has missed our weekly calls."

Shit.

"Five calls, Cole!" she exclaimed. "And you only texted me on two of the others! I've been going out of my mind with worry."

"I'm sorry, Mom," I said. "I was busy yesterday and forgot. I've been working with the Gold and then there was an issue with the ranch—"

"Nope."

I blinked, unlocking the door to my condo and pushing inside. "What?"

"You didn't forget," she said. "You're seeing someone."

"Mom—"

"Shitcan the excuses and tell me the truth. Who is she? Or he?"

"Not a he," I said, then immediately realized my mistake. I'd just confirmed there was a woman. "Or a she. There's not anyone."

"Oh, *there's* a she." My mom sounded positively gleeful at the prospect of someone in my life. Part of me didn't blame her. I'd dated around a lot when I was younger, trying to ignore the draw I had to Olivia. Then I'd swung the other way, becoming almost celibate while trying to regroup and figure out what I should do with my life when it was clear Olivia wasn't on the table.

But now she was and—

My inner monologue had lasted too long because my mom screeched into my ear, "*Oh my God!* You've finally found a good one!"

I winced, pulling the cell away while she carried on. My mom was a lot of things—hard-working, fun, kind—but she was not and had never been quiet. When the noises eventually stopped erupting from the speaker, I put it back up to my ear. "Mom."

I heard a zipper in the background. "I'm coming up to meet her."

"*Mom.*"

"I'll be on a flight later this afternoon."

"M—"

The line went dead.

"Fuck," I muttered, setting down the bag of groceries I'd bought on the counter and typing out a quick text to Olivia. The flight from San Diego was barely more than an hour, add in packing time—my mom would make sure that was minimal—

plus check-in, security, and boarding, and she'd be here by early evening.

Not the way I'd wanted to spend my night.

I loved my mom, was glad to have her visit, but Olivia and I were still figuring things out. I wanted them to be rock-solid before I put her under any scrutiny, so for my mom to come up at that moment was—

Fuck.

An unneeded complication.

I struggled for a minute to find the right words.

My mom is unexpectedly in town and wants to meet you in real life, rather than just on the phone. If it's too much, I'll put her off. If it's fine, come to my place for dinner.

Clunky, but hopefully the correct thing to say.

I put the groceries away, dealt with some emails, then a few problems at the ranch. No response to my text. But I told myself she was probably just busy, so I buckled down and did other things. I spoke to Dev about another new endorsement deal, got it on the schedule, ordered some shit on Amazon that Olivia had at her place so my condo would feel less frat boy and more homey for her. Then I threw some steaks—three. I threw *three* steaks because though I was worried it was too much, I was still hopefuly—into some marinade and stuck them in the fridge.

It was when there was still no response from Olivia, when I dialed her number and was sent straight to voicemail that I realized the three streaks were probably optimistic.

Too much.

Too fast.

Pushing when I promised patience.

Fuck. I'd seriously fucked things up.

NINETEEN

Olivia

MY EYES BURNED, my throat felt like I'd gone down on a flamethrower, and every muscle in my body ached.

Also, I'd broken a heel.

Thankfully, not on my Louboutins, but then again, that was what I got for not wearing my favorites. But I'd switched—unhappily—to the emergency flats I kept in my purse and had taken a Lyft to Cole's place anyway.

I needed to talk to him, to keep the courage I'd found in Dr. L's office and lay it out there. See where the chips fell. Yes, I was pretty certain he was in the same boat as me, emotions-wise, but I couldn't lie and pretend I wasn't praying that the reason he'd stuck was because he loved me just as completely.

But I also knew that sometimes life just didn't work out.

The difference was I'd learned many things about myself over the last month and a half, had them reinforced by Dr. L and Becca, and even Cole, with his patience and care. My past hadn't made them change their opinions of me and it hadn't made them like me any less. Even after I'd told Becca everything, she hadn't looked at me like I was bad, just as when she'd told me about her depression, I didn't think less of her. Why I'd never put the pieces together in that way, treating myself with the same courtesy as I would treat a friend, I didn't know.

All I *did* know was that when Dr. Larsen had pointed it out during that first session, after I'd laid everything I could think of on the table, including Becca telling me her struggles then giving me her appointment time, I'd sat back on the couch, stunned.

"Why does Becca have more worth than you?"

Because I'm not good inside, I'd wanted to reply.

But I hadn't. I'd bit my tongue and thought, quiet and hard and long. Because I knew I *wasn't* bad inside, because my mother's voice in my mind was fading. Being with Cole, seeing him look at me like I was good, had reminded me of the way my dad had loved me. It was painful in a way, ripping off a Band-Aid and exposing my wounds to the air.

But it was also good.

Because I wasn't locked up and shut down. I was finally opening myself up.

No, I wasn't finding my self-worth in others. Instead, it was almost like a fog was clearing and I could finally see myself clearly—flaws, positives, silly quirks, and all.

So, when I had eventually replied to Dr. L, it had been, *"She doesn't."*

And I think it was the first time in my life I'd meant it.

But finding the courage to bare myself to Cole wasn't so easy. He meant . . . everything. I wanted him quite desperately in my life, and also knew that it would up the stakes and change everything.

"That, unfortunately, is the risk we all take with relationships."

Yes, it was.

And I was done with this waffling, scaredy-cat bullshit.

I'd trusted my instincts for years . . . and today I'd trust them with Cole.

Nodding to myself, I got out of the Lyft and strode through the lobby of his complex. I needed to talk to him about my past, let him know I was working on opening up, but that our road would be far from bump-free. And . . . I had to tell him that even though I was a work in progress, I was still a catch he'd be lucky to have, and so he needed to watch his step.

Once a confident bitch, always a confident bitch.

But at least this time, my confident bitchiness wasn't a shield. It was who I was inside.

Bitch—some said it like an insult.

Me? It was a way of life. I could be strong and speak my mind. I could be tough, not take any shit. But I could also be soft and allow someone into my heart.

And I could also want to be loved for all of those things.

Smiling, I rode the elevator up to his place, glad the key fob he'd given me recently made it easier. I'd protested, thinking I wasn't the kind of girl who would use it to just pop in. But then again, I seemed to be exceeding all of my expectations lately.

The doors opened with a faint ding, and I turned to the right, hurrying to Cole's condo.

I wanted to kiss him. I wanted to talk to him.

Then I wanted to kiss him some more.

I knocked, because despite my progress, I still wasn't quite ready to barge into his condo.

"I've got it," I heard a feminine voice call from inside.

Frowning, I leaned back, double-checked the condo number. But, no, this was Cole's place. And then it was too late. Footsteps echoed through the floors, the lock was undone, and a beautiful woman with a full head of blonde hair and warm brown eyes opened the door.

"Hi," she said, startling me with the sheer volume of her voice. It was loud. It was cheerful. It was *a lot.*

I blinked, mentally shook myself. "Hi. Um, is Cole here?"

"Cole, sweetheart," the woman called. "It's for you." Then she took my hand and tugged me inside. "I'm Penny."

I frowned, head tilting to the side. There was something familiar about her voice.

"I'm Olivia."

"Olivia!" she exclaimed and then I was being hugged by a beautiful woman who was in Cole's condo. A beautiful woman who was leading me around like she'd been here many times before, who was comfortable in his space. My throat constricted. My stomach tied itself into knots.

Had I misjudged this entire situation?

Were Cole and I not—

Of course we weren't. I might love him, but our actual relationship had spanned less than two months.

He'd never made any promises in return.

Oh, I was such an idiot.

She squeezed a little harder and, reflexively, I wrapped my arms around her in return. Anything to end the contact. Anything to make it so I could get the hell out of this condo.

That loud, booming voice gentled as she stepped back and looked me over, kindness in her gaze. "It's so nice to finally meet you in person, sweetheart."

In person. I frowned, opened my mouth to—

The pieces finally clicked.

Sweetheart.

Honey.

Blonde hair.

Brown eyes. *Warm,* brown eyes.

Oh.

She'd looked so young on a quick glance, but there were fine lines around those eyes, a faint smattering of creases on her forehead, a few strands of gray hidden in that blonde hair. She was so beautiful that I hadn't realized at first.

She was Cole's mom.

"I love your son."

It was a blurt.

"Did you say something—?" An ill-timed blurt that was punctuated by Cole coming out of the hall bare-chested, his bottom half wrapped only in a towel. He froze, took one look at me and his mom, and I saw the panic ripple across his face.

I was enjoying the view but definitely didn't enjoy the panic.

Or not *much*, anyway.

"This isn't what you think it is," he said.

I fought a smile. "You mean, you wrapped only in a towel, a beautiful woman who's not *me* making herself at home in your condo?"

He paled.

"Or you springing a visit from your mom on me without warning when I look like this." I pointed to my face, no doubt still reddened and puffy then my shoes, the despicable flats.

I watched the relief course over him as he closed the distance between us. "You're beautiful no matter what you wear," he murmured. "And maybe you should check your phone, honey. I left you messages." He took me in his arms.

"Oh."

"Plus, she sprung it on me, too." His lips brushed against mine—

Click.

We both jumped, and Cole glared over at his mom. "Really?"

She patted both of our arms. "You'll thank me later. You two go talk. I'll fix dinner."

"Mom—"

"Shh," she ordered. "Go on." But as Cole took one of my hands, she grabbed the other and squeezed lightly. "Cole's right, sweetheart, you're beautiful." Another squeeze. "Inside *and* out."

Instantly, my eyes filled with tears, my head starting to shake.

She released my hand to cup my cheek, and I understood in that moment where her son had learned to be so wonderful. Her smile was wide and a little mischievous. "Ask my son if you don't believe me. But I'm kind of an expert on people. And you're a good one."

I surprised myself by dropping Cole's hand and wrapping my arms around her.

"Thank you for saying that," I told her. "You can't know how much it means to me." Penny's expression was gentle when I pulled back. "Just know that normally I'm not such a sappy mess. It's just that your son stole my—"

"Oh, for fuck's sake," Cole muttered.

"Heart."

He sucked in a breath.

I went on, "And that I finally found the courage to tell him."

Penny nodded. "You love my son."

Cole's jaw dropped open at her nonchalant declaration, but I found that I liked Penny immensely and didn't care too much that she'd spilled the beans. Hell, I was the one who'd gone full-blurt first.

Plus, now the pressure was off and—

"Right. That's enough." Cole took my hand, started tugging me toward his bedroom.

"You two take your time," she said. "I'll just holler when dinner is ready."

"I think you should go *out* to dinner, Mom," Cole called. "Or maybe back to San Diego until *you're invited*."

"Cole McTavish," Penny and I both exclaimed at once.

Everyone froze.

Only Penny and I began laughing.

Cole just glowered at us.

"Right," Penny said. "I think I *will* catch that last fight of the evening." She walked over to her purse, picked it up, then snagged her jacket from a hook on the wall.

Cole growled, started towing me forward again, only this time it was back toward his mom.

"Mrs. McTavish?" I asked when we were close.

"Yes, sweetheart?"

"Thanks for raising such a good son."

"*Honey*." Cole's voice raised goose bumps on my arms, but Penny simply pressed a kiss to my cheek then Cole's.

"Bye, dears."

"Mom," Cole began.

"I'm ordering a Lyft as we speak," she said, opening the door. "I'll call you both soon."

Another revelation.

A mom that I hadn't had. And maybe a mom I *could* have.

The door closed as I lost my fight with tears. Cole flipped the lock, took one look at my face, and scooped me up in his arms.

Then carried me to his bed and held me as I cried.

And even for a tough bitch like me, that was enough.

TWENTY

Cole

REELING.

I was reeling.

She'd told my mom she loved me, had hugged her with tears in those pretty blue eyes, was letting me hold her while she absolutely lost it.

And she loved me.

Holy fucking shit, she'd finally said she loved me.

I'd expected hard, to have to coax and grind and pull that feeling out of her. Definitely, to have to say it first. I'd even been trying to plan the perfect moment to tell her—one where she couldn't run off in a panic. Instead, she'd just offered it up.

In front of my mom.

Somehow, why didn't that surprise me?

I didn't realize I'd chuckled aloud until Olivia glanced up at me with watery blue eyes. "Why are you laughing?"

"You. My mom. Why isn't it surprising that you two would get along?"

"We did team up well over the phone," she said, tapping her

finger on her chin, before giggling. "I didn't realize you were a glutton for punishment. Sure you want two of us conspiring in your real life?"

Though her question was light, I could still see the hesitation in her eyes, knew that while something had happened today to open her up, it wasn't the be-all and end-all. She'd need patience and understanding. And maybe a little teasing back.

"Do *all* the heels come with you?"

The tension in her shoulders relaxed. "That, and I think I have a hankering to buy more."

"Hankering? You've been to the ranch once and are already going full cowgirl on me?"

She used the back of her hand to rub the tears from her cheeks. "No," she said, and sucked in a breath, releasing it slowly. "I'm coming to you as a girl who grew up off the grid, who was homeschooled most of my life, who only went to real school for kindergarten and first grade—at least until I was fourteen and left home so I could go back. I'm coming to you as a girl who heard her whole life that she was a burden and unlovable." She sighed. "I'm coming to you as a woman who's just started to finally believe that all of those old patterns were bullshit and realizes she has value."

"Honey," I began, but she shushed me.

"I saw Dr. L again today," she murmured. "And she convinced me to lay everything out to you. That's all of my shitty past, and while I try to not let it bleed over to my life now, it still does." She patted her chest. "But I'm *still* me. I'm strong. I won't let it stop me from living, and"—her voice dropped —"from hopefully having you in my life."

"Olivia—"

"But I'm still a work-a-holic who loves shoes," she said over me. "I'm still a tough bitch who won't give you an inch. I want that to be enough for you." Another breath in and out. "But if it's not, I know I'll still be okay. Because I'm also coming to you as a woman who is a fighter, who can endure, who will find my way out to the other side." A beat. "Only this time, I won't have a half-life. *I'm going to have it all.*"

I tugged her back down against my chest, wrapping my arms tightly around her, rocked to the core, unable to know where I should begin when I had so many feelings twisting around inside me.

"I like the heels," I murmured, starting with perhaps the least important fact. But she huffed out a laugh and pushed lightly against my chest, gaining enough distance so I could see her eyes when I told her, "And I love you, honey. Have for a long time, just didn't think I had a chance with the brilliant, hilarious, beautiful woman who I was lucky enough to have in my life. I forced myself to be content with whatever you were willing to give, never knowing that you'd give me *this.*"

"I'm not ever going to be an easy woman to love."

"Horseshit." I sat up and pressed my lips to hers. "The loving part is as easy as breathing. It's all the rest of it that's tough."

"If you're referring to my heels, then I'm going to punch you," she said.

I grinned. "I was referring to us getting out of our own way enough for us to realize how lucky we are to have each other in our lives."

"Oh."

I nipped her bottom lip. "Yeah, *oh.*"

Her hands drifted to my towel. It was precariously perched around my hips, and having my beautiful woman sprawled on top of me meant that it wasn't covering much of my growing problem.

I stopped her, just for a moment.

"Honey, we both know that life throws us curveballs, that

bad things happen to good people, and that there will always be bumps in the road." Her fingers clenched into fists, worry creeping into her eyes. "But there is *no one* I would rather share those rough patches with than you."

"I'll keep going to Dr. L," she said. "I'm going to keep talking through my past, make sure I'm not the one creating those patches."

I shook my head, cupped her cheek. "You'll keep going to talk to someone as long as *you* want, as long as it's helping you. And together, we'll do our best to pave our own road, okay?"

She sighed. "Why do you have to be so logical and smart?"

"I've been around you too long."

Olivia grinned. "I love you. Now"—her fingers slipped from my grip and went back to work on the towel—"tell me you love me, too or I won't go down on you."

"*Honey*."

She glared, though her lips were twitching.

"You should know by now," I said, flipping us and unbuttoning her pants, fingers slipping between her thighs.

"Know what?"

"That I don't come first."

And then I kissed her, knowing that things might never be smooth or easy or bump-free, but so long as they were spent with Olivia, rough, bumpy, and tough would be just perfect.

"I love you too, honey."

EPILOGUE

PART ONE

Olivia

I CLOSED the door to Dr. L's office, feeling exhausted mentally, but also lighter. The burdens I'd shouldered for more than twenty years were getting lighter and while I still went backwards sometimes, still retreated into my shell, the six months of therapy coupled with the six months of Cole, had made a huge difference.

Becca sent me a text when I'd hit the street, asking about dinner that night since the guys were off on some man's trip, fishing in a cold-ass river somewhere up north.

I'd grown up off the grid, had hardly spent a moment with clean clothes or nails or even a clean face, but I drew the line at spending overnights in freezing cold water casting a fishing line for naught.

Want to come to my place? I have the playpen Jasper can crash in. Then you won't have to clean anything up.

That was another part of the new and improved me.

Friends. Or at least being open with them enough to have a crib folded up in my closet . . . or well, in Cole's hall closet, since we'd moved in together.

Weekdays in the city. Weekends and holidays at the ranch.

It was working. It was us. It—

He'd sacrificed his second bedroom to my clothes and shoes. Though, not without a fight. Later, I'd realized he'd only been trying to rile me up so I'd get angry, we'd fight, and then we'd tear our clothes off during makeup sex. But since the makeup sex was hot as hell, I'd decided to forgive him.

That and because I'd come home the following weekend to find all my clothes and shoes organized by color and season.

It was kind of nice having a house husband. Or a part-time one, anyway, since he was helping develop the youth program for the Gold and still involved with the ranch— which was up and running, the first summer of camps a roaring success. They were working on expanding the program to include more year-round programs, but for now, the team was happy with their first run.

Your place sounds perfect.

I smiled, gave Becca my ETA, and hustled back to Cole's place. We'd order in, I could snuggle Jasper, and then watch the latest pop star documentary on Netflix. It'd be great, especially if I could coax a little wine into Becca.

She was a total lightweight and her tipsy commentary made for a giggle-inducing night.

I stepped off the elevator and walked down the hall, keys out. But when I reached the door to the condo, it flew open and I was yanked inside.

"Sweetheart!" Penny's voice boomed as she wrapped me in a tight hug.

I didn't jump because I'd gotten used to her volume, but I did hug her back because I'd learned that not much felt better than having Penny McTavish hug me tightly.

"This is a surprise," I said.

She didn't do surprise visits—or even ones that she sprung on us—any longer. There was always a call a few days or weeks before.

"Are you okay?" I asked.

Penny nodded. "Fine, sweetheart. I had some business in the area, called Cole, and found out you were here, so I thought I'd make dinner and hang out a bit."

"That sounds wonderful," I said and meant it. "Becca and Jasper are coming over."

"Jasper?" Penny smiled. "That little boy is so stinkin' cute. Come on," she said and took my hand, tugging me further into the apartment. "Get out of those clothes and into something more comfortable. I'm making pasta."

"On it." I strode toward the second bedroom, now my closet, and began changing, but when I stopped by the master to grab my phone charger, I froze.

"Penny?" I asked, heart thumping in my chest.

We hadn't filled the walls yet, both having been so busy and neither of us being able to agree what should go on them—though I think I mentioned my stance on arguing about silly things and the subsequent greatness of makeup sex.

But there was something on them now.

Pictures.

A huge portrait of Cole and me staring into each other's eyes from that night six months before, when we'd finally laid it all out. Shots of us since then. Us smiling at the ranch, Bucky in the background. Holding hands on the beach, the sun setting behind us. Me sleeping on his chest. Him holding a fishing pole.

Memories.

Good ones.

Penny wrapped her arm around my shoulders. "Are you mad, sweetheart?"

I shook my head. "No, Penny. I-it's wonderful."

My life with Cole out there, full and happy and so much more than I ever could have hoped for.

"I didn't mean to find the ring," she said. "I swear. I was just snooping through Cole's drawers, trying to find a warm pair of socks, and—"

I twisted, jaw dropping open. "What ring?"

Penny's eyes went wide. "Oh shit."

"I meant the pictures," I said slowly. "He bought me a ring?"

More wide eyes. "The pictures are lovely. Did he just put them up?" she said, trying to steer me away from the bedroom. "Sauce is on the stove. Bread's in the oven—"

"Ring?" I asked again, just as my phone buzzed.

I can't decide if I want you to love the photos or hate them so we can have more makeup sex.

Penny bit her lip.

I showed her my phone.

"Yes," she said, chagrined. "I found a ring."

We both looked at each other and laughed. Then the doorbell rang, and Becca came in, carrying a babbling Jasper, baby bags tossed over both shoulders. We were relieving her of them when the timer on the oven went off and then we spent the next few hours scarfing down food, getting Jasper to bed then drinking wine and bingeing Netflix before we were all too tipsy and tired to go anywhere. So then we spent a while getting Becca settled in the spare bedroom with Jasper, and Penny comfortable on the couch when she wouldn't sleep in my bed.

Thus, it was much later by the time I found a moment to text Cole back.

I love the pictures and I love you.

Also, I'll never turn down makeup sex.

His response made me smile as I careened headlong into sleep.

Honey.

Yeah, things might not be perfect.
But they were damned close.
And that was everything.
Plus, he'd bought me *a ring*.

EPILOGUE

PART TWO

Artemis

HE DIDN'T KNOW I was a woman.

That was wont to happen with a name like—

"Artie?"

I didn't hold it against the young male director for staring around the room—devoid of people except for the two of us—in confusion for several long moments. With a name like Artie, I was often confused for a man. Especially considering that I was in the movie business, and specifically production, which was a male-dominated field.

Though I had to give it to him, he recovered quickly.

His smile was charming, his looks even more so, but I was going to give him bad news.

I couldn't stand his films.

Any of them.

He was talented, an up and coming young director who could barely grow a beard, but he had vision, he was smart, and he could shoot a movie.

They just weren't for me.

And so I was going to pass on this project.

Probably stupid, considering he was going to be the next hot thing in Hollywood, but also that was me—not the stupid part, but the going with my heart and gut and *never* working on a film that I wasn't passionate about.

I'd promised myself that before getting into the industry and I'd kept that promise for the last sixteen years.

Films that showed women in strong, fulfilling roles. Films that featured talented female comedians. Films that featured all colors, genders, and sexual orientations.

Films that weren't Hollywood.

It wasn't pandering. Audiences understood when they were being played.

They also understood genuine.

I'd built my career on that notion and I'd become successful. But it had taken a solid ten years of working and hustling—and did I mention *hustling*—before I'd gotten well-known enough that I'd actually made so money.

And also four Oscars, but I didn't need to brag.

Snorting to myself, I lifted my brows and my glass to my lips.

"You're Artie," Pierce Daniels, said handsome, young director, answered his own question and sat in the chair opposite me, extending his hand for me to shake.

The contact sent a zing up my arm, made my heart skip a beat.

Uh-oh.

ACTION SHOT
NOW AVAILABLE

Artemis and Pierce's story is now available. Get your copy at
www.books2read.com/ActionShot

LOVE, CAMERA, ACTION

Dotted Line

Action Shot

Close Up

End Scene

Blocked

Backhand

Boarding

Benched

Breakaway

Breakout

Checked

Coasting

Centered

Life Sucks Series (**all stand alone**)

Train Wreck

Hot Mess (coming soon)

Roosevelt Ranch Series (**all stand alone, series complete**)

Disaster at Roosevelt Ranch

Heartbreak at Roosevelt Ranch

Collision at Roosevelt Ranch

Regret at Roosevelt Ranch

Desire at Roosevelt Ranch

Phoenix Series (**read in order**)

Phoenix Rising

Dark Phoenix

Phoenix Freed

Phoenix: LexTal Chronicles (**rereleasing soon, stand alone, Phoenix world**)

From Ashes

In Flames

To Smoke

KTS Series

Fire and Ice (Hurt Anthology, stand alone)

Stand Alones

Someday, Maybe (YA)

ABOUT THE AUTHOR

USA Today bestselling author, Elise Faber, loves chocolate, Star Wars, Harry Potter, and hockey (the order depending on the day and how well her team -- the Sharks! -- are playing). She and her husband also play as much hockey as they can squeeze into their schedules, so much so that their typical date night is spent on the ice. Elise changes her hair color more often than some people change their socks, loves sparkly things, and is the mom to two exuberant boys. She lives in Northern California. Connect with her in her Facebook group, the Fabinators or find more information about her books at www.elisefaber.com.

facebook.com/elisefaberauthor

amazon.com/author/elisefaber

bookbub.com/profile/elise-faber

instagram.com/elisefaber

goodreads.com/elisefaber

pinterest.com/elisefaberwrite

www.ingramcontent.com/pod-product-compliance
Lightning Source LLC
Chambersburg PA
CBHW031022260626
47153CB00018B/2775